PERDITA'S PASSION

PERDITA'S PASSION

Genevieve Lyons

Chivers Press • G.K. Hall & Co.
Bath, England   Thorndike, Maine USA

This Large Print edition is published by Chivers Press, England, and by G.K. Hall & Co., USA.

Published in 1998 in the U.K. by arrangement with Severn House Publishers Ltd.

Published in 1998 in the U.S. by arrangement with Robert Hale Ltd.

U.K Hardcover ISBN 0–7540–3274–4 (Chivers Large Print)
U.K Softcover ISBN 0–7540–3275–2 (Camden Large Print)
U.S. Softcover ISBN 0–7838–8459–1 (Nightingale Series Edition)

Set in 16 pt. New Times Roman.

Printed in Great Britain on acid-free paper.

British Library Cataloguing in Publication Data available

Library of Congress Cataloging-in-Publication Data

Lyons, Genevieve.
    Perdita's passion / Genevieve Lyons.
    p.   cm.
    ISBN 0-7838-8459-1 (lg. print : sc : alk. paper)
    1. Large type books.   I. Title.
    [PR6062.Y627P4   1998]
    823'.914—dc21   98-5510

This book is for my lovely friend Barbara Westerberg who introduced me to the Brooke Hospital for Animals upon which the Cooke Hospital in this book is based. They do the most wonderful work in Egypt and Petra and all around the Middle East. I would like to thank them for their help and wish them well for the future in their wonderful work.

And to my beloved daughter Michele.

CHAPTER ONE

As the clergyman said the words, 'I now pronounce you man and wife,' Perdita saw Larry turn away from his bride and look over his shoulder directly at her.

She was just behind the bride and groom, decked out in her finery. 'Like a bloody Christmas tree,' she thought.

Posy had chosen the dress, a frilly pink number that was not at all Perdita's style. She felt uncomfortably aware that neither the colour nor the cut suited her. She looked, she decided, like part of the wedding cake.

She stood rooted to the spot clutching the bride's bouquet, white-knuckled as if she was in the dentist's waiting room.

Larry had to turn quite awkwardly to see her. Why had he done that? It embarrassed and excited her. Struggling as she was with her feelings, trying so very hard to accept the fact that he was marrying someone else, she had psyched herself up for this day. Since last he held her in his arms, she had relegated him to another compartment of her mind; a sealed compartment. She had demoted him from passionate lover to friend and that was so difficult, and very, very painful.

It was odd, she thought, how she could go on doing normal things even when momentous things were happening. Even while her heart was breaking she ate, blew her nose, coughed, swallowed.

She was a spunky girl. She was a survivor; someone who struggled to conquer her emotions, not allow them to dominate her. She was used to doing these things, managing herself, and even though her heart was broken her stern upbringing prevented her from what her mother described contemptuously as 'going to pieces'.

It had to be faced and she faced it bravely, full-on, even though the pain in her chest threatened to overwhelm her. The man she loved so passionately, the only man she had ever loved, would ever love and whom she had thought loved her was marrying Posy Gore, her best friend. How could that be? Why had he deserted her? What had she done? Where had she gone so wrong that he was marrying someone else?

And Posy? What was Posy thinking of? Were they really in love? Did Larry love Posy, then, more than he had loved her? It seemed impossible, yet at the moment when he had uttered the most sacred words, the clincher words, the binding-together words, he had turned around in the church and looked at *her*.

Had Posy noticed? Perdita was not sure, it had happened so quickly, was over in a flash.

The church was full of light. The sun shone as if a film director had arranged it, in shimmering rays slanting directly on to the bride and groom, spotlighting them. Perdita heard Larry's cousin, Leonard Dalton, a photographer by profession, murmur, 'Lovely, lovely, oh boy that's perfect, perfect, perfect!' as he snapped the event for posterity. There was another professional somewhere with a camcorder whirring away.

The church was packed with well-dressed, stylish people with happy, smiling faces. Some of the women, mainly the married ones, were dabbing their eyes with tissues or handkerchiefs, depending on their ages, very careful of their make-up. Each recalling, sentimentally, their own wedding day, those days in their lives when everything seemed perfect, when the world was full of hope, their hearts full of love and the future stretched before them, unrealistically trouble-free. Only Perdita struggled. 'Oh God, help me to stop loving him,' she prayed as the organ crashed out Mendelssohn's *Wedding March* in triumphant crescendo.

Posy's veil was back now and as she turned she smiled radiantly at Perdita, accepting the return of her bouquet from her friend's outstretched hands. Was there a hint of victory in Posy's eyes as she smiled at Perdita?

Larry was not looking at her now, but he was not looking at Posy either. He was looking at Leonard who was snapping away, dancing backwards down the aisle. The 'someone else' who was capturing it all on video whirred away just behind him and Perdita flinched as his lens pointed towards her face. She did not want to be captured forever on tape looking pained and tense, her eyes full of anguish. To be frozen like that forever, with her feelings naked on her face, would be awful.

They went out into the sun, the organ music ringing in their ears. Rice and confetti were thrown. People laughed and squealed excitedly. Everyone seemed happy, full of good humour, only Perdita ached for it all to be over.

She thought, despondently, that she would have to sit at the wedding feast, keep smiling, keep up the act for another couple of hours at least. Was she capable of that? The pain inside her twisted her heart, tightened her throat and made her head throb unmercifully. It was the first time she had seen Larry in months and she had not known it would be so agonising. Every lovely curve of his face, every precious bone in his body was so very dear to her, so familiar, so beloved. How could she live without him? I know every inch of you, she thought, I love every tiny bit of you, so how did this happen? I thought you loved me. Oh God, Larry, I believed you loved me with the same passion that I loved you. Well, she thought, I was wrong. So wrong.

The village church was very old, chosen for its quaintness. Posy was not a very religious person. She stood under the apple trees by the lych-gate, her arm through her new husband's, smiling up into his face and Perdita hoped vindictively that an apple would fall, plonk on top of the bride's head. But it didn't. Her wish went unanswered and Leonard and some of the camera-mad crowd click-clicked at Posy's laughing face.

Then she too turned and looked over her shoulder at her friend, at Perdita. The russet leaves drifted down like the confetti all around her and this time there was no mistaking the look of triumph she shot at Perdita, no mistaking it at all. 'I've got him,' her expression said, 'You haven't!'

As Perdita stared at her friend, her father came up behind her. The sound of his voice in her ear startled her.

'Let him slip through your fingers, eh Perdy?' he remarked. 'Bloody careless of you!' Perdita shivered. How was it he always managed to hurt her, always managed to say the one thing that would pain her most. 'You do not look your best, my dear, in pink,' he continued. 'You shouldn't have allowed Posy to put you in that particular colour, and that dress makes you look like a cream-puff!'

Perdita squeezed back her tears. He could still do it. Still hurt her, his words slicing through her, cutting, cruel. I should be used to it by now, she thought, I should, after twenty-five years, have developed some kind of immunity.

5

And I thought I had. But I'm so vulnerable today, so very raw. Perhaps I should not have come.

And where's David? she wondered. And Fern? Surely they should be here too.

She blinked her eyes rapidly and swallowed. She could see the glamorous figure of her mother talking to Leonard Dalton near the ancient church porch. He was snapping her and she was laughing, saying something flattering to him no doubt, but she had one eye on Perdita's father, Lucas. She too seemed vulnerable, Perdita thought. Distressed. There was a wild look in her eye that was quite out of character. She wants him to notice her, Perdita decided, but he won't be impressed. He'll disappoint as usual. Her parents were often not on speaking terms.

Her mother did look beautiful. Stunning really. She always made Perdita feel awkward and unworthy. She wore black and white, a huge-brimmed black straw hat, like a halo in a Byzantine icon. It had a white grosgrain ribbon around the crown. She wore a white silk dress with a black rose print and a black silk swagger coat, short and fluid over it. So chic!

Perdita did not reply and her father moved away. He was flirting with Vicky Mendel, a girl who used to be at school with Posy and Perdita. Vicky had blossomed, there was no other word for it; bloomed and blossomed.

In the dim and distant past Vicky had been

6

overweight and spotty, thick-bodied and unattractive and she had, naturally or by dint of ruthless dedication, Perdita was not sure which, turned herself into a page three girl. Literally. Perdita's eyes had nearly popped out of her head when, over a commuter's shoulder on the tube one day, she caught sight of a near-naked babe, full page in his newspaper and thought there was something familiar about her. The man was drooling over the photo of the topless girl and, craning to see the name, Perdita had instantly remembered. How could she ever forget? Vicky Mendel the ugly bully had turned into this curvaceous chick. The ugly duckling had become a swan. Well, maybe not a swan, Perdita reflected, a pouter pigeon might be nearer the mark. There she was in the paper, re-packaged, bare breasts proudly aimed at the reader, a saucy grin on her face.

Perdita had told Posy the awesome news, that Vicky Mendel was a page three girl, but Posy took the information calmly saying, yes, she thought everyone knew.

'How'd you expect me to know?' Perdita had asked crossly, 'I don't read that paper!'

And Posy had said, 'Well, neither do I, but it didn't surprise me!' and Perdita realised that Posy had not known about Vicky but for some reason had pretended she did.

She looked now with distaste at her father preening before the sexy, big-breasted girl. A contemporary of his daughter. The fact did not seem to bother or deter Lucas Hastings. He wore on his face that buccaneer grin that made him what the BBC called 'the thinking woman's crumpet'. Not that Vicky Mendel could by any stretch of the imagination be called a thinking woman.

'Your father's playing true to form,' her mother's voice in her ear made Perdita jump. 'Who's the girl?' she asked.

'Vicky Mendel. From school,' she replied reluctantly.

'You mean that chunky little bully you and Posy hated so much? The one who didn't get to go to see Lucas on his programme?' Perdita nodded. 'Well, well, well. She did finally get to meet him,' her mother's voice was waspish. 'She looks like a tart and is behaving like a tart, so she probably *is* a tart!'

'Oh Mother!' Perdita's tone was resigned. She was used to her mother's caustic comments, her father's put-downs yet they always affected her. She wished she could develop a thick hide, that what her parents said would cease to hurt so badly, that so many relatively unimportant things would cease to *matter* to her so much. The smallest thing, she reflected, threw her, building up real or imagined slights into agonizing facts.

They were piling into the cars now. Leonard took Perdita's arm. 'Come with me,' he invited, 'you look quite lost there, all alone.'

'Oh Leonard!' she felt herself wilting before

him, her brave facade crumbling.

'That bad?' he asked. She nodded. 'Larry?'

'Oh yes,' she breathed in painfully.

'Your dad?'

'Mmmm.'

'Your mother?'

'Mmm. Oh, everything. Everyone.'

She looked up into Leonard's kind sympathetic face. 'It's awful! Life sucks!'

Leonard smiled. He had a nice smile. She wondered why she could not fall in love with him. Why, oh why did it have to be Larry Burton?

Leonard took her arm. 'Come on,' he said. 'It will pass. I promise.' He cocked his head. 'I'll drive you to the Savoy. You can cry as much as you like in the car.'

The wedding party was to be held in the Savoy, in the River Room overlooking the Thames. Perdita was only too happy to go with Leonard. It removed her a little from the main protagonists, gave her a little space.

Leonard's car was around the side of the church. Green velvet fields stretched away to the horizon and here and there little cottages snuggled into the land looking serene and somehow reassuring. They had been there for so long, surviving wars, love, hate, family tragedies and dramas and celebration. The message was, as Leonard said, that everything passes. Except property. She thought of Oak Wood Court and sighed.

Perdita smiled at Leonard. 'I'm grateful,' she said as they got into the car and fastened their belts.

'It's okay,' he replied turning the key in the ignition, glancing at her. 'You still love Larry, don't you? Even though . . .'

'Oh yes, I still love him, Leonard,' she turned away from him, looking out of the window, 'I didn't know till today how much.'

'What went wrong?' he asked. She shrugged.

'I don't *know* what happened. It's a mystery.'

'You don't, eh?' He sounded disbelieving. He backed the car out of the lane and began to drive towards the motorway.

She stared at him. 'Do *you* know, Leonard?' she asked.

'Well, I think . . . See I tried to guess. I've written the scenario. You fell out of love with him . . .'

'Oh no. No, no, no!' There was pain in her protests.

'Well, I thought maybe you'd thrown him over, and then, obviously Posy moved in. I didn't believe that Larry would be such a fool not to get wise to Posy. She's so transparent. But Larry is old fashioned.'

'What do you mean, Leonard? I don't understand.'

'What a perfect couple you and Larry would make. You're as innocent as he is. How two such bright people can be so naïve I don't know!'

10

'What do you mean?'

'Oh, Perdita, everyone knows it except you. And maybe Larry. Posy wants to *be you*.' He bit his lip and glanced sideways at Perdita. 'I think she's pregnant,' he said.

Perdita frowned, digesting this. 'Larry's baby?' she asked in a choked voice. 'Ah, Jesus!'

Leonard swung the car around the corner leading to the motorway. That would do it, she knew, for Larry. He was so chivalrous, so conscientious. He would insist on being responsible. But she couldn't believe it. That meant he'd had sex with Posy when he was supposed to be loving her. But Leonard continued. 'I wouldn't put anything past her. She may be lying.'

'Oh, Leonard, don't be so unkind,' she protested but it was automatic.

'Well, it's true. Little Posy gets what little Posy wants come hell or high water, haven't you noticed?'

'Not particularly. She's always been a good friend to me,' Perdita had said this so often it sounded like a mantra. 'When I was lonely and had no one . . .' her voice trailed off.

'You are *too* loyal Perdita,' Leonard said, and then, frowning, 'Now shut up and let me concentrate on my driving.'

They were on the motorway. Perdita could see the large black limousine with the white ribbons fluttering from the bonnet ahead of them. It was going to be a long day.

She sat back and lapsed into silence and allowed Leonard to get on with it. She thought, remembering their lives together, so entwined, that Posy had indeed always been there. Always.

CHAPTER TWO

Perdita remembered when she first saw Posy Gore, the very first time she had really noticed her.

Posy was sitting on the low bench in the school changing room clutching a shoe-bag. She was staring at the milling throng of uniformed teenagers around her with wide, frightened eyes.

They were changing for gym and Perdita felt a tug of pity for the small girl sitting there as if frozen to the spot.

'Hey, you new?' she asked. The girl looked up, nodding. She had scared eyes and a hungry expression.

'She left me here,' she whispered and Perdita could see she was scared. 'And I don't know, I don't know . . . what . . . where . . .'

'Here, let me help. You must have Anna Dent's locker. She left. Her parents are in the Dip Service. Most of the girls here have parents overseas.' Then, seeing the bewilderment on the girl's face she explained. 'Diplomatic

Service,' she said.

The stranger nodded. 'I know. My father is ambassador to Mhulendi,' she stared at Perdita. 'It's in Africa. He doesn't want me there because he says the schools are not up to scratch. Is your father in the . . .' she paused, glanced shyly at Perdita, 'the, er, Dip Service too?'

They giggled together at this and Perdita shook her head. 'No, my father is a TV presenter. Lucas Hastings.' She always sighed when she imparted this piece of information, expecting the awed response. Posy did not disappoint. 'God! You mean *Lucas Hastings*! On the BBC? *Lucas Hastings* is your *father*?'

'Yeah.'

'Holy mackerel!'

The girl introduced herself as Posy Gore and latched onto Perdita instantly and forever. It seemed natural for Perdita, after their meeting, to show the newcomer around, explain the routine of the school to her. She showed the new girl the ropes and found that Posy clung to her like ivy.

Perdita did not mind and they became friends. Indeed she was grateful for she had no friends of her own anyway.

St Catherine's was a fashionable private boarding school. Most of the girls there had parents abroad. Perdita's parents, however, had sent her there not because they travelled but because they did not really want her around.

'Father says it's for my good, that this is the best school in England,' she told Posy, 'but he can't fool me. He just doesn't like me much. He *hates* my mother.'

'I can't wait to meet him,' Posy said. Perdita looked at her, puzzled. 'Oh, I don't think you will,' she told her new friend, '*I* hardly ever see him myself.'

Posy smiled and did not argue. They lay in the dorm whispering, the curtain between their beds pulled back. Perdita had wondered at the chance that had taken Jessie Lomax out of that bed and into Anna Dent's now vacant one down at the bottom of the dormitory. When she asked Jessie the girl giggled and said, 'That new girl, Posy, gave me a gold chain if I'd move. She must have a pash on you, to think you're worth a gold chain.'

'Oh, don't talk rot,' Perdita had retorted sharply, but it made her think. Then she forgot about it.

'It's a bit thick though,' she told Posy, 'knowing you irritate your father and your mother hardly knows you're alive. We have a house in Berkshire but my father is hardly ever there. Mother is an interior decorator and she has a *pied à terre* in Kensington. Father practically *lives* in the studios. He has a poky little place in Shepherd's Bush.' She shrugged. 'He says he chose it deliberately with no room for anyone except himself.'

14

'My dad is *always* preoccupied,' Posy told her. 'He's got no time for me. I don't irritate him like you said you irritate your father. That at least would be *something*. He's just *worried* all the time. But he smiles. He's always smiling, never stops no matter what upsets we have. Always has this grin on his face, but his eyes are desperate.'

'And your mother?' Perdita asked.

'Oh, Mother is scared too. It's contagious, fear is. Ever notice? If one person is afraid it *infects* others. She doesn't sort of have *time* to be anything but worried. She *says* she worries about me all the time but I don't believe she does. I think she just worries out of habit. She never writes and seldom phones. When I call her she's never there and if she is she only talks for a minute, then says she has to go.' Posy was silent for a moment, then she said 'But I'm going to change my life, see if I don't. I'm going to get everything I want.'

'Oh dear, what a right pair we are!' Perdita laughed. She pulled the curtain across.

'Night, Posy.'

'Night, Perdy.' Silence, then, 'Perdita?'

'Yeah?'

'We're friends, aren't we?'

'Sure,' Perdita was drowsy, wanting to sleep.

'Best, best friends. Friends till death,' Posy insisted.

'Sure.'

'Till death us do part.' Posy's voice was

15

intense.

'Of course. Now let me sleep,' Perdita yawned and drifted off into oblivion.

It was nice to have a friend. Perdita was a lonely girl. Neglected by her parents, until Posy came on the scene she had spent most of her time by herself. She did not make friends easily and being Lucas Hastings's daughter did not help.

She had inherited her mother's beauty and her father's intelligence and a lot of the girls were jealous of her. Though she did not impress or startle at first glance, hers was a beauty for the connoisseur. Wonderful bones, elegant lines, a Filippo Lippi Madonna. She was tall and rangy and, horror of horrors, could eat what she liked without putting on weight. It was perhaps this more than anything else that made the others reject her and hold her in suspicion.

She got firsts in her exams without too much swotting and that did not help either. So, in spite of the fact that such a girl was, in books, the favourite, the leader, in real life Perdita found she aroused only resentment and envy.

Another thing that aroused their animosity was the fact that all the girls wanted her to get them tickets for various TV shows; chat shows to meet their favourite pop stars, game shows to win big prizes and make an impression, and simply to be invited into the glamour (as they thought) of the studios and the media people.

16

They could see no reason other than sheer meanness why she wouldn't accommodate them. Her father had the number one show on telly, and they simply did not believe her when she told them that her father wouldn't oblige.

Lucas Hastings refused point blank to get tickets for anyone, ever. He was adamant. So Perdita had to tell her fellow students and classmates that her father did not go in for that sort of thing, but they didn't believe her.

'If he once started,' she told them, 'he says the demand would never end. He decided he wouldn't ever make an exception for anyone, ever.'

The girls refused to understand and it did nothing to help Perdita's popularity.

Perdita did not help matters herself by not appearing to care. A little display of vulnerability or need might have softened hearts which were intrinsically hard, but she was fiercely proud and refused to stoop to subterfuge to gain friendship and acceptance. Besides, she had been rebuffed by her parents and knew the hurt of rejection, and so she guarded herself against it.

Posy filled an empty space in her life and if she was not the ideal companion, someone Perdita would have chosen for herself, nevertheless Perdita was glad of her friendship.

There was one girl, large, unattractive and a bully, who hated the tall leggy blonde and who relentlessly played tricks on Perdita, generally endeavouring to make as much mischief for her as possible. Perdita tried not to allow Vicky Mendel to get to her. Underneath, Vicky, like all bullies, was weak and had an inferiority complex.

Perdita was stronger both mentally and physically but she was incapable of using the sort of tactics, the show of strength needed to stop Vicky and her little set.

Besides she was so used to her father and mother verbally abusing her to be able to ignore the girl's vicious tongue. But until Posy's arrival at St Catherine's Perdita had combated Vicky Mendel's persecution, taunts and tricks with the same method she used on her father and mother: by pretending nothing was happening. She simply did not react.

Just suffered. Suffered dreadfully. Most nights she lay crying into her pillow, careful that no one heard her, loneliness engulfing her in waves. But she would not crack. When Posy came she had someone to share her suffering with and it made a huge difference. And Posy chose to remain staunchly at her side against the crowd. Perdita could not understand why, but she was very grateful.

Vicky had a gang and after Posy's arrival it seemed her sole purpose was to torment the two friends. Their schemes became outrageous and, angered that Perdita had an ally, the gang poured gallons of water on the friends' beds so that they had to sleep in wet beds for weeks.

They filled the lockers beside their beds with new-born mice from the lab and their gym shoes with the contents of a jar of sauce from the kitchen.

It infuriated and frustrated Vicky that neither Posy nor Perdita were intimidated. They did not respond or let their taunts appear to hurt, treating the pranks and insults with lofty disdain. The girls did not seem to care if everyone thought them chicken when they refused dares. And all the time Posy was there, by Perdita's side, together with her in unpopularity.

Posy wanted to go to Oak Wood Court, the vast estate that old Jack Armstrong had left to his daughter, Perdita's mother.

'I've read all about it in *Hello!* magazine,' she told Perdita, 'Oh please, please, please invite me! I'm your best friend, aren't I?' She nagged and nagged until eventually Perdita asked her mother if she could bring her friend for the weekend.

'Of course, darling. But I do hope she'll know how to conduct herself. Who are her people?' This was the kind of remark that made Perdita reluctant to have Posy stay with her. Her mother, and her father, could make a person feel very awkward indeed. Perdita, however, had underestimated Posy.

'The Gores. Her father is Ambassador in Africa,' Perdita told her mother.

'The South African Ambassador? White I

presume?' and without waiting for a reply, 'Oh, that's fine. I'll be there this weekend. I have to check up on the drapes in the library and Bates says the Persian carpet has caught the sun in the music room and there's a faded patch. Some silly maid forgot to close the shutters. So I'll see you then. Graham will pick you up in the car.'

*   *   *

The school was not too far from Oak Wood Court, both being in Berkshire, and to Perdita's great embarrassment, Posy squealed in excitement when she saw the Rolls in front of the school entrance awaiting them, and Graham in full uniform holding the back door of the car open.

'Oooh Perdy! This is style! This is so cool!'

'Don't, Posy, *please*! It's too *gross*. It's *not* cool to go ballistic about a *car*. Unless it's a Lamborgini.' She sighed. 'Mother insists that they'll treat me better in the school if she flashes a bit of money about.' Perdita rolled her eyes to heaven. 'If only she knew! It makes them *hate* me. It's trashy to flash. Not the thing at all!'

Posy never oohed again in Perdita's presence, even though the grandeur of Oak Wood Court far exceeded her expectations.

They sat in the rear of the Rolls as it bore them smoothly up the driveway to the mansion surrounded by the wonderful hundred-year-old trees the place was named after. Posy could not restrain a gasp when the house hove into view. It was a gracious building: Corinthian pillars fronting a terrace that looked out over the lawns; the dolphin fountain in the middle; the rose garden to the right and the oak wood to the left. It conveyed a sense of permanence, an indifference to time, serene and classic, impervious to the hassles of the world.

'It's beautiful, Perdita,' Posy breathed. She felt nervous now with the reality of wealth and privilege palpable in front of her, and she felt the stirrings of misgivings.

Melinda met them on the terrace. A man servant took their cases from Graham and disappeared with them into the great marble hall Posy could glimpse through the open front doors.

It was June and warm for the time of year and Melinda sat at the table on the terrace. Her greeting for her daughter was coolly distant and she welcomed Posy graciously but without warmth. She was, Posy thought, the most elegant and sophisticated woman she had ever seen in her beige Armani trouser suit and cream satin shirt, her grooming impeccable.

They sipped tea and nibbled cucumber sandwiches in silence. Melinda made absolutely no attempt at conversation. Posy, it seemed to Perdita, dwindled visibly in her mother's presence and she did not blame her friend. Posy seemed to shrink into her chair as if she wanted desperately to disappear and shook her head every time she was offered anything by the immaculately uniformed Filipina maid.

'Well, if you are finished Maria will show you your room, em, Posy,' Melinda said at last, not really looking at her guest and Posy squirmed in her chair, wishing now she had never asked to come here, wishing she was a hundred miles away. 'She's in the Yellow Room, Perdita.' Then Melinda suddenly stared at the guest. 'Maria will have unpacked for you. You'll find everything ready.'

Melinda pressed a bell beside her on the white damask clothed table and Posy thought about her jumble of packing, and the state of her underwear and felt herself shrink under the stare.

In moments another Filipina maid appeared from the house.

'Take Miss Gore to her room, Maria.' Melinda glanced at Posy again. 'I don't suppose you have appropriate clothes to dress for dinner,' Melinda said calmly, looking her guest over, 'but we do dress for dinner here so do your best. Perdita will lend you something. Everett Nash is dining with us and Lydia Beckworth.'

'Oh, Mother, Lady Beckworth is absolutely *horrible*!' Perdita cried, 'Why did you have to ask her? You know I hate her.'

'Well, you'll have to put up with her this evening. That's what society is all about. Putting up with people you don't like and never allowing them to suspect it. Shows how well-bred you are.' She sipped her tea and Posy did not know whether to rise or stay seated. She was acutely self-conscious and felt as if she was six times larger than normal.

Melinda's perfect face was without feeling. There was no shadow of joy or warmth to be found there, no glimmer of a smile broke the severity of her expression.

'Doctor Lovette is coming too, Perdita. Try to entertain him,' she looked at Perdita, then Posy. 'Perdita is not at her best entertaining,' she said, 'she does not have the social graces and I'm sure I don't know *where* I went wrong. My husband says it's all my fault! I hope you are more gifted, Posy, in that direction.' She sighed. 'Well, perhaps Perdita will improve when she gets out of these terrible teens.'

She beckoned with a slim white hand and the maid drew near. 'Maria,' she said then turned to Posy. 'They are *all* called Maria. It's an obsession with them.' Then turning back to the maid, she said, 'Please take Miss Gore to her room. Be down at seven-thirty for eight, Posy, please. Drinks in the library. All right, off you go.'

'You never *told* me,' Posy said when Perdita came to her room half-an-hour later carrying an evening dress over her arm.

23

'I *did*. I did, I did!' Perdita cried, 'I told you over and over and over but you didn't *listen*!'

'It's so unfriendly! The house is a mausoleum.' Posy shuddered. 'It's scary.'

'Well, I warned you but you *would* come.'

'I thought your Mum and Dad might be a bit stand-offish, like in *Murder on the Orient Express* or *Death on the Nile*, but this is . . .'

'Well, I live with it,' Perdita said tartly. 'Here's a dress of mine you can borrow. Don't thank me either, I'm cross.' She went to the door and turned. 'This weekend is going to be a disaster, I can feel it in my bones. But then, all my weekends are disastrous, so what's new?' And she left Posy alone.

The rooms were coldly austere, Posy discovered. They were as unwelcoming as the hostess and Posy found the great house intimidating. But she was impressed and determined to fit in. She decided she could get used to the grandeur and formality of Oak Wood Court and decided to become a constant visitor there.

Perdita told her that her mother insisted on keeping everything as Grandfather Jack had had it, refusing to change anything. 'It's a shrine,' she told Posy, 'and that's why I think Father is uncomfortable here.'

Posy succeeded in her plan. She cultivated Melinda who was not impervious to her outrageous flattery. Posy instinctively knew how to ingratiate herself when she wanted. She had that social ability that Melinda derided her daughter for lacking, and that Perdita was too straightforward to manage. Posy knew how to please those who might be useful to her, aware of their unspoken needs from a light for a cigarette, a refilled glass to the right thing to say and when to listen and murmur assent. She was adept at massaging egos and persuading people of their own importance.

Perdita was not so gifted and often fell foul of her mother's acid tongue. There, too, Posy was sympathetic. She consoled Perdita often when her friend was reduced to tears at some carelessly cruel criticism made by Melinda.

So Posy overcame her nerves and often visited Oak Wood Court. She was very disappointed, however, that Lucas Hastings was never there.

'Doesn't Mr Hastings ever come down here?' she asked one evening when they were dining, just the three of them alone. They were in the library sipping sherry, Melinda was of the school that believed young people should be broken in to the social graces as soon as possible. Perdita had been allowed small quantities of alcohol since she turned twelve. 'A sip of wine or champagne never hurt anyone,' Melinda said. 'Nobody *likes* the taste at first so best to get used to it early on.'

Posy had never had alcohol before she came to Oak Wood Court and she loved the taste from her first sip. But she did not tell Melinda that. She was far too clever.

There were usually dinner guests at Oak Wood Court and sometimes house guests and Posy liked that too, although Perdita hated it. Posy had to pretend to her friend that she too was put out by the visitors, but in fact she adored the challenge of winning them over, of getting them to notice and like her.

And they did. They liked her because she made herself useful to them. She agreed with them. She flattered them.

But that night there were no visitors. Melinda had not expected to be there and was not in a good mood.

Losey, the gardener had told Bates the major-domo who had informed his mistress by fax to London that a strange sickness had attacked her roses and they needed specific treatment.

'I need her to see for herself. Decide which way to go. Won't take the responsibility on my own,' Losey said.

If Melinda cared for anything apart from Lucas it was her roses. She loved that garden, its bowers, its arbours, the overwhelming scent, the beauty of the blooms. So she had come down to make her choice of cure for her darlings' sickness. She was worried more about their health than she would have been if Perdita had been ailing, and Perdita was aware of this.

Melinda was also cross for now she would

miss the first performance of a new production of *Aida* at Covent Garden. Perhaps the Vicky Mendel situation would never have been resolved for Posy and Perdita if Melinda Hastings had not been so angry.

'No he doesn't, the stupid man,' she replied to Posy's question about Lucas not coming to Oak Wood Court. She sounded more acerbic than usual. 'Don't sit like that, Perdita, you look like a farm labourer.'

'Sorry, Mother.' Perdita sat up straight on the leather chair.

Her mother always asked her to sit there and she always slid down and her mother always corrected her.

'How many times must I tell you?' Melinda asked rhetorically. 'No, Lucas does not come to Oak Wood Court very often which is funny because it was one of the reasons he married me,' she said bitterly.

'Mother, please!'

'Everyone *knows* Perdita. Besides Posy is almost one of the family. I only wish you had half her social graces.'

'It's so sad I've never met him,' Posy interpolated hastily. She was thrilled at Melinda's words but anxious not to upset Perdita. The last thing she wanted was for Perdita to go off her.

'Oh! Celebrity hunting, Posy?' Melinda hit out, accurately, to Posy's discomfiture. But Posy shook her head vehemently.

'Oh no! It's just that,' she leaned confidingly towards Melinda, assessing her anger and the perfect climate for her plan, 'remember how we told you about Vicky Mendel?'

Melinda nodded, 'She sounds very ill-bred,' she remarked, 'not at all the thing.' But she was not very interested.

Posy said, 'Well, she's getting worse. She's doing filthy things now. Tell your mother, Perdy.'

'Oh, it doesn't matter,' Perdita said briskly. The last thing she wanted was to get her mother involved in school upsets. She only managed to make things worse. Melinda had an awkward habit of marching into the school, throwing her weight about, metaphorically speaking, and threatening Mrs Pollock and making everything impossible.

'Tell me, Posy, if my daughter won't.'

'I just think it is best ignored. We are not reacting to her disgusting tricks so she'll get tired. Eventually.'

'Yes. And maybe she'll have really hurt us by then,' Posy said, 'who knows what she'll think up next? See, Mrs Hastings,' Posy turned to Melinda, 'she put urine in Perdita's water. The glass we have beside our beds at night.' Perdita looked out of the window, her face stony. Melinda looked horrified.

'But that's revolting! And dangerous. Outrageous. Why didn't you tell me, Perdita? I'll go back with you tomorrow and speak to

28

this girl. And Mrs Pollock. I'll get Lucas to sue. I'll create such a scandal. I'll make a real stink . . .' Perdita sighed. 'I told you,' she whispered. But Posy protested aloud.

'That would only make it worse,' she said, shaking her head. 'No, Mrs Hastings, I have the perfect answer. Settle it all peacefully. No trouble. Only I don't think you could manage it,' she said slyly.

Melinda's eyes glittered. It was a challange that Posy could not have put better. Perdita stared at her in admiration. Posy launched into her master plan. '*All* the girls want to see the TV studios. The BBC. They would *adore* to see your husband's show. It would be *educational* too. So, if Mr Hastings could let Perdy and me bring our friends, that is all the class *except* Vicky Mendel and her cronies, then I can guarantee they'd never bother us again.'

'*I'll* get you tickets,' Melinda said firmly.

'But Father will be—'

'Your father need not know anything about it. I'm his *wife* after all. I'll tell them it's to be a surprise. His daughter's class. Sure.' Melinda sounded as if she would enjoy it, but Perdita sat horrified at the scenario that flitted through her mind. Her father would be furious and her mother would not be there.

'I wonder, could you get *two* sets?'

'Why two?'

'Oh, Perdy, don't be dense! We'll only ask our friends the first time. But we'll let it be known that Vicky could persuade us the second time . . . the carrot, see?'

'Dangle the possibility of a later visit to the Beeb depending on behaviour? You are a clever minx, Posy. I think I'd rather have you as a friend than an enemy,' Melinda said dryly.

'But I'm not hurting anyone. I'm being a peacemaker,' Posy said virtuously.

'But Mother, Father will be—'

'Don't worry about your father, Perdita,' Melinda said, the light of battle in her eyes. 'Leave him to me.'

*   *   *

Melinda was, if the truth be known, delighted to have this opportunity to spite her husband. She had suffered so many slights, smarted under his indifference so acutely that she looked on this as a heaven-sent situation; a chance to get at him whilst helping her daughter. She got two sets of tickets behind her husband's back. She sent them to St Catherine's with instructions to allow Perdita and her chosen friends to go to the show.

Lucas's programme was a mixture of political cut and thrust, investigative reporting and interviews with the current names in Government, the literary world, the arts, film and pop worlds. It was presented in front of a live audience and Mrs Pollock, the headmistress, decided in her wisdom that the show would be an educational experience for her pupils.

Suddenly Perdita was the most popular girl in the school. She gave the list of names of the people she was inviting to the headmistress and noticed the flicker of understanding cross her face as her eyes travelled down the names. She knows, Perdita thought. She knows something has been going on and she hasn't done anything about it. She stared at the headmistress in disgust until the latter said, 'Fine, Perdita. This is fine.'

'Everyone's going from my class, except Vicky Mendel,' Perdita said pointedly. But Mrs Pollock did not pick her up on it. 'Vicky Mendel is not invited,' Perdita added.

'Very well, the choice is yours, Perdita,' Mrs Pollock replied and that was that. 'You may go, Perdita, and remember I expect you all to behave like ladies.'

Fifteen girls went to the show. Lucas was infuriated but, daunted by the horde of teenagers, he simply ignored them, leaving them to the ministrations of the hospitality staff.

The girls had a ball. They met a politician, which bored them, but Mrs Pollock would be pleased to hear about it. They met a superstar promoting her latest film who was delighted to spend a little time with them. Their obvious admiration repaired somewhat the damage Lucas's abrasive questioning had done. Last of all they met their dream-boat, Oggy Vac Two from the Hot Bed Bash, the very, very latest cool pop group. They gawped and sighed and he signed their autograph books, for he too felt a little squashed after his interview with Lucas Hastings, though unlike the film star he was not bright enough to fully comprehend the derision and contempt that he had been held up to.

After that, Vicky Mendel lost her gang. The other girls blamed her for their lack of invitation. The second tickets were never used, for Lucas Hastings issued a ban on anyone under eighteen being allowed into the audience. He announced that he was concerned about the morals of the young and his show, he insisted, was adult and sometimes contained unsuitable language. 'A load of crap,' was how his daughter summed it up.

*   *   *

'See,' Posy said, 'she knows now she's no match for you.' She was referring to Vicky.

Perdita shrugged. 'She never was,' she replied calmly, 'she was never worth bothering about. All her pranks were so *feeble*.'

Posy said, 'I think you're wonderful!'

Perdita said nothing. She did not want to be thought wonderful but it seemed ungracious to say so. She knew the truth; that she *wasn't* wonderful. Posy had this weird idea about her that she was special. But Perdita knew better.

32

Her mother and father were really clever people and they found her a big disappointment. They could not be wrong. Posy, after all, was immature. What did she know?

She had taken Posy very much for granted and now, sitting in Leonard's car she thought about her in a detached way for the first time. Had she really thought Perdita was so wonderful? Why on earth had she invited Perdita to be her bridesmaid? To the wedding at all?

And Vicky? Why had she invited Vicky to her wedding? Perdita recalled that after the visit to the *Lucas Hastings Hour* Vicky had sucked up to the friends and, whereas Perdita had kept her at the usual arm's length, Posy had basked in being wooed by the girl.

Now Vicky was flirting with Lucas. Well, Perdita thought, she'll suffer for that. Lucas will flirt back and then, without conscience, he'll discard her. No matter what happened, Vicky would suffer. Her father made everyone suffer.

Vicky was someone else now, not the girl who bullied herself and Posy. That was another time, another world.

Leonard drove in silence, the car rolling smoothly towards London and the Savoy and Perdita took off the horrid little bunch of organza flowers and rested her head on the back of the seat, and remembered.

CHAPTER THREE

She wondered when it was that Posy had begun to copy her. Posy's hair was wild and fluffy and dark but she had at some time cut it, had it straightened and dyed blonde. It did not suit her. The shoulder-length cloud of dark hair had haloed her small face, given it definition, while the flat blonde bob diminished her. When she came to think about it, Perdita realised that Posy wore her uniform the same length, wore her cardigan over her shoulders the way Perdita did, oh, and lots of other things. She wondered now why she had not thought it odd before.

Posy insisted on flattering her even though Perdita would shake her head and deny the compliment. 'Oh don't talk tosh, Posy. I'm *not* beautiful. You know I'm not. Lucas says I'm the ugly duckling that *won't* turn into a swan.'

'Oh, your father's an artist. He's creative,' Posy told Perdita earnestly, 'it's to be expected from him. Creative people are difficult. And destructive.' She nodded wisely.

'And you would know, would you? Well, let me tell you, not all of them are, not by a long chalk. I can count—'

'Well, he *is*!' Posy interrupted firmly, 'so you must forgive him. But that's not the point. The

34

thing is, you are beautiful and the others are jealous. Why else do you think they're so cool with you?'

'I don't *know* Posy, and I don't *care*. Let's leave it. Okay?'

The uniform thing seemed silly at the time. Perdita's uniform was short on her because her legs were so long. Posy had hers taken up to thigh-length and Vicky Mendel had pointed it out to her one day after choir. 'Your friend looks like your clone,' she whispered in Perdita's ear on the way out. 'Same uniform, same hair.' And then, some weeks later, after Posy had read an Andrew Marvell poem aloud in class, Vicky had mouthed, 'Same voice!' Posy had finished so Perdita didn't think about it, brushing it off. She felt it necessary to stand up for her friend against the enemy, as she then thought of Vicky, denying any accusations she made, even to herself. She would always be loyal.

'Why doesn't your mother divorce your father if she hates him so?' Posy asked after the show when they had all seen Lucas Hastings at his most vitriolic about his wife.

'You got the tickets from *whom*?' he had shouted, and when Perdita told him he yelled in disbelief, 'From *her*! Bitch! She'll pay for this. Your mother, Perdita, is a shit of the first order, a harridan and a trollop. Be warned! If you turn out like her you'll end up in the gutter. It is where she should be, would be only for me.'

The girls all thought this outburst the artistic temperament in full flow and they shivered with excitement and wished that their dull, dreary fathers showed such spunk. Perdita hated it and wished she were somewhere else, anywhere else. 'My mother won't divorce him,' Perdita said, 'and she doesn't hate him, she loves him.'

'Funny way of showing it,' Posy said, bewildered.

'No, *he* hates *her*,' Perdita tried to explain. She knew Posy would never understand the complicated relationship. 'He won't divorce her because she has the money and the house.' Posy would understand that. 'But I think that underneath it all they really love each other. I think they *enjoy* fighting. I think they get a kick out of it.' She frowned, and added, 'It makes me sick, though.'

It was her dream. She wanted so desperately to believe that the acrimony, the fights, the verbal abuse was a game, that Lucas and Melinda loved each other really and that they both loved her but had a funny way of showing it.

She had fantasies in which she would have, say, a car accident, or nearly drown. She would be doing something very brave, like swerving to avoid a child or rescuing a friend from drowning. She would come to in a hospital bed and there on one side would be her mother and on the other her father. Melinda would be weeping, concerned and devastated and Lucas, eyes full of tears, would smooth her damp hair back off her forehead, tenderly, lovingly. 'You gave us such a fright, Perdita,' Lucas would say and her mother would nod. 'Don't ever do that to us again,' Melinda would sob, 'We love you so!' and Lucas would nod. It was her favourite dream, treasured, consoling, nurtured at twilight, and after it she always slept soundly.

Melinda was an interior decorator. Lucas said she was an inspired amateur. 'She has no training in design or at *anything* to qualify her for the job,' he would say disdainfully. 'I don't hear any of my clients complain,' Melinda would reply tartly.

'That's because anyone who'd have you for a designer must *per se* be clueless,' he'd retort triumphantly.

When Perdita left school her mother gave her a job in The Design Factory, her firm, and Perdita got a tiny little flat in Chelsea. She was glad to get away from the quarrelling, the dissension, to be private, uncriticised, at peace. She didn't put much effort into the little two-roomed flat. She looked on it as a temporary place of peace, a break from Berkshire, from school, from Oak Wood Court and Kensington before she moved on somewhere else. She had this feeling that she was marking time, that something would turn up to change her life. The clouds would lift and she would suddenly know what she wanted to do, which direction her life would take.

When her mother asked her how she had decorated the flat Perdita tried to explain this feeling to her, but her mother said, 'Nonsense, Perdita, you'll still be here in twenty years' time, wondering where your life has disappeared to. You have absolutely no ambition.' Her mother did not bother to come and see the apartment and Perdita was just as pleased that she did not.

On one of the rare occasions that Lucas was at Oak Wood Court, Perdita had cause to think about her friendship with Posy analytically. She tended to accept the girl's presence without question, but Melinda, with her usual acidity, remarked, 'Are you two joined at the hip, or what?' when Perdita pitched up with her friend for the weekend.

It was autumn and they sat around the long heavy mahogany table eating a salad lunch.

Posy was there as usual. Posy was always there. Perdita did not answer her mother but it started a train of thought. It was automatic now, Posy coming to Oak Wood Court, Posy keeping her company wherever she went. Perdita wondered now why.

She supposed she used Posy as a buffer between herself and her parents, yet very often Posy agreed with them. It was habit, Perdita decided, and what other choice had she? Posy admired her; or said she did.

Neither Lucas nor Melinda seemed surprised at the girl's constant presence, but although Posy's affection and admiration was balm to Perdita's deprived soul, it also irritated her and made her uncomfortable. It was as if she did not *deserve* Posy's friendship and also she did not completely trust it.

She was not sure if this disbelief sprang from her own insecurity or suspicion that maybe Posy was a sycophant, that she was as Lucas, cruel as ever, would say, arse-licking.

It was Lucas who brought to their attention the fact that Posy was utterly without family or friends.

'Seems strange,' he muttered that autumn day over lunch in the dark, heavily Victorian room. 'You'd think you could dredge up an uncle or an aunt, a cousin maybe. *Someone!*'

Posy shifted uncomfortably on her chair. Melinda often asked why she bothered to come to Oak Wood Court and put up with the baiting that went on. Posy never replied.

'Well, I . . .'

'Her mother and father rarely come to London,' Perdita said.

'They were both of them only children,' Posy added.

Then Lucas looked down the table at his wife. 'I believe,' he said, 'the Design Factory is not doing so well,' he remarked with relish. The girls on either side of the table between them stared from one to the other.

'It's the Nineties, Lucas,' Melinda replied tartly, 'or haven't you noticed? I thought political commentators like yourself were supposed to notice social changes? When I started the business fifteen years ago people could *afford* to have their homes "done over" as the Americans say.'

Lucas threw a glance at the ceiling. 'Ghastly American vernacular,' he remarked.

'But they can't now. These are more frugal times, Lucas, and DIY is the thing these days.' She smiled down the long table at him. 'But I'm still doing reasonable business.'

'And you have, my dear, enough money of your own to be able to afford not to worry about trivialities like lack of customers.'

'Precisely!' Melinda went on smiling. 'And,' she announced, 'With Perdita, in the Factory alongside me—'

'You're working with your mother?' Lucas gasped. 'Dear God, I knew I'd bred a dud but you really are proving a total wash-out Perdita if you settle for mindlessly titivating inanimate objects for tasteless clients in bourgeois houses.'

'That kind of sentence *may*, I repeat *may* impress on your programme, Lucas but it leaves me totally unmoved,' Melinda retorted, 'I make a good living at it—'

'Huh! Your clientele has halved in the past five years.'

'One exclusive client per year is enough to

keep me busy,' Melinda bit her words off, two spots of red on her cheeks.

'He's getting to her,' Perdita mouthed at Posy across the table.

'Unlike you, Lucas, my work does not depend on ratings.'

'Just as well for you, my dear, if it did you would have to shut up shop.'

'My work has appeared in *House and Garden,* and in *Hello!* magazine!' There was a note of childish pride in her voice.

'Oh halleluiah! The zenith of style and artistic achievement. *House and Garden*! *Hello!* magazine! Oh, bully for you!' Then he glanced at Perdita. 'I suppose you realise you'll be her slave labour. She can't find staff because she is an appalling boss so she'll pay you a pittance to be her gofer, run errands, be general bloody dogsbody.'

'No, Father, I don't think so.'

But Lucas was right. Melinda behaved as if Perdita was still in the nursery and she could order her about willy-nilly. She had her daughter doing errands that a child of ten could easily manage and although Perdita asked regularly, pleaded with heartfelt passion for more responsibility, Melinda promised but never fulfilled her pledges.

And so it went on and Perdita whispered to herself in the dark of the night, they really do love each other. They're just playing a game. They really do love me. I'm not a wash-out, someone to be despised, to be looked at with contempt, not worth knowing, not able to do much more than run errands.

And Posy told her she *was* worthwhile. She supported Perdita, bolstering her confidence, what little she had.

Then, that weekend Posy asked Melinda for a job in The Design Factory. And got it.

'I do hope you don't mind, Perdy. We're best friends and I want to be *with* you. It would be such fun, wouldn't it, working side by side? And I'm sure I could help you with your mother.'

'You could have told me you were going to ask her.' Perdita struggled with her feelings. She did not want Posy in the shop but she was sure her antipathy at the thought of working with her friend was based on jealousy and unworthy emotions and only a real bitch would mind her friend working alongside her.

'Well, I *was* going to tell you, Perdy, but then I thought, Mrs Hastings won't want *me*!' Posy laughed self-deprecatingly, 'She'll turn me down flat, never let me work with Perdy. It's a wonderful dream that'll never come true. I'd've told you and then I wouldn't have got the job so we'd *both* be disappointed.'

She assumes I want her to be there, Perdita thought, biting her lip, feeling like a louse. Oh God! I'm *horrible*!

Perdita had met Posy's parents only once. They had visited London from Mhulendi when the girls were still at St Catherine's. They had taken the girls to tea in the Savoy. Mr Gore smiled all the time, just like Posy said he would and Mrs Gore stared at him, stared at Posy, and stared at her. It was very disconcerting. She seemed to be waiting for something all the time. Expectant.

'Posy says you are great friends,' Mr Gore remarked. Conversation was stilted in the extreme. He seemed to be at a loss to know how to talk to his daughter which, Perdita reflected, was only to be expected. He never *saw* her. There were long silences in the Savoy lounge.

'Yes, we are Papa,' Posy cried eagerly.

'Good, good.' Another long pause.

'You happy about that?' Mr Gore asked Perdita who didn't know what to say so she nodded.

'Your father is Lucas Hastings?' Mrs Gore enquired.

Again Perdita nodded. 'That's nice,' Mrs Gore remarked then lapsed into a brown study of her husband's face.

Mr Gore suddenly said, 'We called her Posy because she was so sweet. Like a bunch of flowers. When she was a baby.'

Mrs Gore nodded eagerly, 'Yes, yes. We didn't know what to call her for *weeks*. She had no name, poor little scrap. Then her father said, "She's like a posy of flowers", and from then on it was Posy.'

'Yes. Like a bunch of flowers when she was a baby. Then she grew up,' Mr Gore said. 'I suppose it's a silly name now,' he smiled dryly. 'Oh no!' Perdita protested. Another silence. 'You like school, do you?' This from Mrs Gore. The girls nodded and Perdita gave up and looked around.

All the other people there seemed at ease with each other. They laughed while they nibbled their sandwiches and scones. The pianist in the arbour in the centre of the room played Cole Porter.

Thick carpets absorbed the sound of footsteps and waiters flipped efficiently about and the clink of china and the buzz of conversation made a pleasant background for the elegant crowd. But not for the Gores or Perdita. At their table the awkward silence persisted.

Perdita remembered that day now as she got out of Leonard's car on Posy's wedding day. That day so long ago when they emerged from the Savoy and waved the Gores goodbye, Perdita remembered Posy looking back over her shoulder at the gracious facade. 'When I get married, Perdy, I'll have the reception here,' she had affirmed. And she had been as good as her word.

Perdita remembered saying, 'How do you know you'll get married, Posy?' and Posy's reply, equally firmly, 'Oh, I will. I will.'

Perdita had not thought about Posy's parents

since that day when they had tea together. They were shadowy background figures, but, she suddenly realised, they should be here now, surely, on their daughter's wedding day? She had not noticed them in the church and she looked around but could not see them anywhere here either.

Lucas was sitting in a comfortable armchair, his nose almost buried in Vicky's cleavage. Staff were hovering over him as if he were royal or something. He always commanded this kind of attention and Vicky was obviously revelling in it. Perdita glared at him bitterly then, turning, noticed her mother doing exactly the same thing; glaring at Lucas.

Perdita frowned. Her mother looked as if she was going to cry, and Melinda was always so in charge of herself. Perdita's heart skipped a beat and for a moment she felt frightened and she didn't know why. Such naked pain on her mother's face took her aback.

Posy beckoned her over. She sat at the head of the table, Larry beside her. The wedding breakfast was about to be served. The table was covered in white napery, champagne bottles on ice, white flower arrangements, glimmering glass. Behind her, Perdita could see the slow, sinuous grey scarf of the Thames flowing past and in front of her the guests were taking their places, searching for the placements.

'Perdy, I wanted to thank you, thank you very, very much,' Posy looked at her most

45

sincerely.

'What for?' Perdita asked. She would not look at Larry. She could not bear to. He sat with his back half to them, speaking to Leonard.

'For everything. Your friendship. All those years. For everything you did for me, all your kindness.'

'For Larry too?' Perdita could not resist asking coldly.

Posy's eyes widened and she drew in a sharp breath. A look of touching innocence settled on her face. 'Why Perdita, what on earth do you mean?'

'You know exactly what I mean.' Perdita wished she could stop. It was an inappropriate conversation at an inappropriate time.

'Sorry, but I don't! I'm surprised, Perdy, after all this time that you could be so, well, I hate to say it . . . bitchy! This *is* my wedding day after all,' Posy looked hurt and reproachful. 'I was your friend all those years when no one else wanted your company . . .'

'What . . .?' Perdita's eyes widened. She stared at Posy, speechless.

'When no one wanted to be your friend,' she repeated firmly. 'I was loyal and faithful,' she persisted. 'And, Larry told me it was all over with you and him. *All over*. So . . .' She shrugged. 'What you expect me to do?' She was whispering, she obviously didn't want anyone else to hear her. 'You can't blame me, can you?

He just got bored with you.'

Sitting there in her white satin wedding-dress, the flowers in hair that was bleached and cut to look exactly the same as Perdita's, the innocent expression was gone and in its place, eyes narrowed, lips drawn back she looked for a moment feral, like an animal with bared fangs and Perdita shivered. She suddenly realised that perhaps she had always known Posy felt like that about her. That underneath it all she really hated Perdita, was jealous of her. The problem was, Perdita always deplored her thoughts when they took that turn, believing she was being, as Posy had just accused her, bitchy. Maybe she *was*. It was all so confusing.

Then as swiftly as the vicious expression had appeared, it vanished to be replaced by sweet serenity.

'We'll say no more about it, eh, Perdy?' Posy asked.

Larry was turning around and the wedding breakfast commenced. It passed, for Perdita, in a blur. She sat beside strangers, aunts and uncles of the groom. This should be my day, she thought, these people my new relations. She felt sorry for her breakfast companions for she was as awkward as the Gores and they laboured in vain to get her involved in the conversation.

Later, someone came to her with a pile of faxes, telegrams, goodwill messages. 'Can you take these up to the top table?' a bright-faced male who was slightly drunk asked. 'And why aren't you there? You're the bridesmaid, after all.' For the first time she wondered about that, then decided it was not worth the bother. What did it matter anyway?

She rose and found her knees unsteady. She must have drunk more champagne than she had intended. She wasn't drunk exactly, but she wasn't sober either.

She moved as steadily as she could to the top table. She handed the pile of paper to Leonard.

'Wonder who they're from?' she said, leaving them on the table in front of him, 'Posy's got no one but me. They'll be Larry's mates,' she added. Leonard looked a bit startled.

'And where is David? And Fern? Where are they?' she heard herself ask, quite loudly. She did not look at Larry. She could not bear to. She wanted desperately to throw her arms around him and ask him what had happened. She wanted to tell him she adored him, that her heart was breaking, but as she opened her mouth someone drew her away quite firmly.

'I want to say ... I want ...' she was muttering, but whoever was steering her moved her purposefully from the top table. She turned to protest and saw the person who had hijacked—or saved—her was Larry's mother.

CHAPTER FOUR

If Perdita's parents battled and Posy's smiled remotely and seemed incapable of communication, Larry's mother, Anjelica Burton, epitomised to Perdita the perfect mother. Kindly, understanding and friendly, Perdita had looked on her as ideal. She had not seen Anjelica since the split with Larry. She had dodged her and not answered her calls. Perdita was not sure why she had acted like this except she believed that somehow she was to blame and that Anjelica would tell her it was all her own fault. Perdita had longed to talk to her lover's mother about the sudden collapse of their relationship, but kept putting it off, in the hopes of . . . what? She had no answer.

Larry's mother was drawing her away now from certain disaster and Perdita knew that she read the situation accurately and was saving her before she made a spectacle of herself.

'You don't want to do or say anything you might regret, Perdita,' Anjelica whispered and sat her down at a table some way from the bride and groom. People were dancing and the band was playing 'I Just Called To Say I Love You.' They were alone at the table.

'What on earth happened between you and Larry?' Anjelica demanded. She leaned forward. 'I've never seen a couple more perfectly suited than you two. Then suddenly . . . this!' she spread her hands and nodded towards the bride and groom.

She was a stout, homely woman with a wide smile and beautiful, kindly eyes. 'That one,' she said indicating Posy, 'is trouble. I was so sure *you* were the one for him, Perdita. You seemed so happy together.'

Tears filled Perdita's eyes. She never cried in public but the champagne seemed to have loosened her up and now she began to sob. Anjelica made her exchange places with her so that she had her back to the newly wedded pair. 'Oh God, I'm sorry,' Perdita blubbered, 'what will you think of me?'

'Hold on, Perdita, I didn't mean to upset you,' Anjelica looked about. 'Calm down and tell me what's wrong. I thought you two were perfect together, and happy.'

'So did I,' Perdita cried, wiping her eyes. It was difficult to stem the flow once it started. 'So did I. Oh, Anjelica, I don't know what happened. It was all fine, I thought. We had pledged ourselves to each other in Egypt. We came home and then suddenly, without a by-your-leave, Mother telephoned to tell me Posy and Larry were engaged. Well,' she amended 'David did first, I think.'

Anjelica's brow furrowed. 'It's so utterly unlike Larry. To behave irrationally, to change his mind. It's simply not his style.' Her eyes hardened. 'And I don't like this one at all.' She indicated Posy, shaking her head, obviously perplexed. 'And where *is* David?' she asked, 'what happened to him?' She spread her hands and Perdita's heart missed a beat. 'He should be best man. After all he's Larry's best friend. Always has been. Hector Davenport has never been that close to Larry. I can't understand any of it Perdita, I really can't.'

'Have you asked Larry?' Perdita queried, not wanting to talk about David.

'Of course I have, but I cannot get any sense out of him.' She took Perdita's hand between hers. 'And I've never seen him so uncomfortable. Never. Larry is an honourable man, he *has* to be true to himself or he's on hot coals. Oh God, Perdita, what on earth's going on?'

Perdita shook her head and did not reply. She liked Anjelica holding her hand. She liked the touch. She wished her mother would make affectionate gestures like that but Melinda never did.

Perdita had a good idea why David was not there. He would not want to see her, or Lucas. She sighed. What a tangle it all was.

'I'm feeling very sleepy, Anjelica,' she said.

'Here, have some coffee,' Anjelica urged, letting go of her hand, filling a cup, giving it to Perdita who gulped it down like medicine. Anjelica refilled the cup. 'Your nerves will be shot to pieces,' she said, 'but it's better than falling down.'

Anjelica leaned back in her chair, staring up at the top table where her son sat with his bride. He was laughing, head back showing his fine teeth, sharing a joke with Hector and Leonard. Posy sat twirling a glass which was empty, staring into space.

'I've never liked that girl,' Anjelica said, then glancing at Perdita, 'Oh I know she's your friend, Perdita, but there's something, well, unpleasant about her.'

Perdita said nothing. She was wondering how she could have been so blind all those past years.

''Scuse me,' she stood a trifle unsteadily, 'got to pee.'

'Let me go with you,' Anjelica said, rising too.

'I'm okay really,' Perdita smiled at Anjelica, 'I won't disgrace myself. Don't worry.' She took a deep breath and walked with great dignity towards the ladies.

She had the sense, when she reached the short flight of steps that led to the upper lounge to hold onto the banisters as she mounted them.

In the ladies she bumped into Vicky Mendel. Vicky avoided her eyes. 'Don't worry about me Vicky, what my father does is of no interest to me,' she told the girl, giggling. Vicky smiled tentatively back at her.

'It's nice to see you, Perdita,' she said. Her eyes were anxious and Perdita realised suddenly that Vicky was in awe of her.

'Well, I don't know if I can return the compliment,' Perdita replied, then seeing

Vicky's crestfallen expression decided, what the hell? It seemed so unimportant now, so trivial. 'After what you did to me in school,' she finished. It sounded feeble to her and the accusation lacked force.

'You were so stuck-up,' Vicky said, 'you were like royalty, exclusive. You and Posy. She never let any of us near you.'

'What do you mean?' Perdita, suddenly sober, stared at her erstwhile enemy.

'Well, like, she told us all about your . . . your . . . well, you know.'

'No, Vicky, I don't.'

'Well, like, oh come on Perdita, *you* know.'

'No, I don't.' Perdita was becoming more and more apprehensive. 'Tell me.'

'That you and she were . . . like a couple. *You* know. She said you loved her,' Vicky sighed, took a deep breath and said, 'that you were lesbians. But you *knew* that.' she muttered defensively.

'No, I did not,' Perdita said quietly, 'and for your information, Vicky, nothing like that went on. I am not a lesbian. I've never *loved*, as you call it, Posy Gore.'

Vicky was staring at her, drying her hands in the towel. 'You mean that . . . you mean she was lying?'

'Yes, Vicky. She was lying,' Perdita said firmly.

'Je-sus! Cripes! We believed her,' she gulped. 'Christ, Perdita I'm sorry. We shouldn't

53

have . . . thinking about it we really should not have taken any notice of what Posy Gore said. She boasted all the time . . .'

'About me?'

'Yeah. About you. She told us how your father and mother fought all the time. How your father made a pass at her one night but she knew you would be wildly jealous so she never told you. Gosh, Perdita, we didn't know she was lying.'

'Okay, Vicky. Enough. I don't want to hear any more.'

'I'm sorry, Perdita, I'm really sorry.' Vicky came over to her and Perdita could see genuine regret in her eyes. 'I was such a stupid cow. Still am. I was jealous of you. You are so beautiful, so . . . so . . . you had everything. I guess if we'd thought about it we'd have realised we were being given a line, but I guess we *wanted* to believe it.'

'Masie Stokes and Jinny McAlister *were* a couple and you never hassled them,' Perdita remarked.

'No. But we weren't looking to hassle them.' Vicky shook her head. 'God, I was a jealous bitch. I know you can't forgive me. I don't *expect* you to. Just the same, I'm sorry.'

'Oh I do forgive you, Vicky. I really do. I was as stupid as you. Stupider in fact. Naïve. A dope.'

'She takes people in,' Vicky said with something like admiration in her voice. 'She's a great con artist, when you think of it.'

'Well, we've got her number now,' Perdita said.

'Not before time.'

They parted, if not friends exactly, at least at peace with each other. The champagne had dulled Perdita's responses and she was not up to piecing what Vicky had told her together and fitting it into the various incidents in their lives. What other lies had she told? And had she perhaps fabricated some fairy tale about her for Larry's consumption? If she had and he believed a slander then Larry was not worth having, not worth loving. But she doubted it very much.

Perdita tried to assimilate the information she had just received after Vicky left the ladies and she sat staring at herself in the mirror while the attendant fussed around her, wiping non-existent specks of dust off the vanity tables, looking at her apprehensively. She sat there until Anjelica, fearing the worst, came to find her.

CHAPTER FIVE

They had had good times together. Posy could always make her laugh. She was much better at the work in The Design Factory than Perdita was. Or so Melinda said. Regularly. 'It's my turn now,' Posy told her. 'You were always helping me with my homework at school. Perdita was so clever, Mrs Hastings,' she told Melinda.

'I doubt it,' Melinda said.

Perdita believed she was clumsy and obtuse because her mother's constant criticisms made her that way. Her mother took away her confidence while at the same time she boosted Posy's. But then, Posy praised Melinda as much as Melinda praised her. It seemed to Perdita as if her friend and her mother were locked in a mutual admiration society and she was left out in the cold. She tried to be grown up about it, but when she tried to have a civilised conversation with her mother about it like they suggested on the talk shows Melinda said she was jealous and denied that she treated Posy any differently to the way she treated Perdita.

'I send Posy off to get me something and she comes back with exactly what I want. I send you ... you never manage to do it right. Never. What do you expect me to do? Give you a medal for screwing up?'

Perdita had screwed up the day she met Fern and David for the first time. And Larry.

By this time Posy had her own tiny apartment. She had wanted to share with Perdita and had pleaded. 'It would be cheaper all round, Perdy. We could get a much bigger flat if we shared.' Then she begged. 'We've been friends for so long, Perdy, why don't you

56

want me to live with you? I've done so much for you, I was the only one who stuck by you all these years.' Then she threatened to break off their friendship. 'Oh, you are being so mean! How can you? I don't think I want to know you any more.' But she did not mean this and it was about this time that she was deciding to ask Mrs Hastings for a job.

Perdita held her ground. She said she needed her privacy. 'It's all you'll get, privacy,' Posy cried, 'you've never had anyone else but me. Never. Even your parents don't like you. You'll regret it, being all alone all the time and you'll change your mind. But don't think I'll come running. I won't.'

They had never been close after that, although Posy kept up the appearance of affection for Perdita. They saw each other daily in The Design Factory, but whatever had tied them together had gone and they only tolerated each other because of their mutual past and because they were used to each other. And Perdita was not lonely in her tiny apartment.

Then the day came that was to change everything for Perdita.

It was a cold March day, sunny but windy. Perdita would never forget that day, the day she met Larry. She would never forget anything about it.

All of London was in bloom. Apple blossom, cherry blossom, the daffodils were everywhere.

Trees heavy with magnolias, waxen pink and white flowers floating in the warm air and every tree bursting into verdant leaf.

Her mother had sent her to Colefax & Fowler on the Fulham Road to match some samples and swatches, and there in the window of a rather expensive but discreet Italian restaurant, she glimpsed her father.

She was going to rush across the street to greet him, something she always did when she saw him even though she knew she would be rebuffed, held at arm's length. She went on rushing into his arms and Melinda said she was a glutton for punishment. That March day she stalled. What stopped her was the fact that she had to wait for a break in the traffic. If the road had been clear she would have run across and the story of her life might have taken a completely different direction.

But the traffic was rushing past, horns honking, and when Perdita, hopping from foot to foot was able to get a clear view she saw her father emerge from the restaurant. And then she saw he was not alone. He had someone with him. It was a woman. A beautiful woman.

Perdita froze. She was used to seeing her father flirt with babes but this was no babe. Melinda was a beautiful woman but few would say she was soft. This woman was soft as butter. She was a curvaceous woman with a wonderfully sexy body. Perdita ran her hands over her own slim figure. She took after her

58

mother, lean and rangy as a boy, a clothes hanger, enviably beanpole tall and flat. This woman was voluptuous. Red-haired, round faced, dimples probably, Perdita hazarded a guess. She looked as if her whole body would be dimpled. She had a tiny waist and inside her wool suit she swelled into curves above and below her belt. The wind blew her hair across her face and Lucas turned and gently lifted the red-gold strands and pushed them back. There was something in his gesture that stopped Perdita's second attempt to cross the road and made her want to hide from them. There was an expression in his face so tender, so loving, an expression that she had never seen there before. They looked as if they were locked in their own world. Very private.

This was not a colleague, no working lunch. And this was not lust, some casual fling with a bimbo. This woman was different.

Perdita got furtively back into her car hoping they would not see her. She hunched over the wheel trying to make herself invisible, heart beating a tattoo in her chest. She felt as if she had peeped into someone's bedroom and seen something she shouldn't. She felt guilty.

She watched them laughing together. Her father looked so handsome and charming when he laughed but it was not something she ever saw him do. This man was the father she had always dreamed about, the sarcastic droop gone from his mouth, the bitterness from his eyes. He was young, boyish and good-humoured as he stood there in the Fulham Road holding this woman's hand, hailing a taxi.

There were a lot of people around and the traffic flowed loudly by, screening her from the couple. She thought of them as a couple. A traffic warden on the prowl was approaching Perdita purposefully so she started the Audi and pulled away from the curb just as a taxi pulled up in front of Lucas and the woman. Perdita, turning the car, saw him help the woman in and they drove off.

She followed them. They turned towards the King's Road in the direction of Parson's Green. They ended up in front of an elegant house in a terrace of elegant houses, a house with window-boxes full of yellow and purple pansies. The taxi drew up and her father and the woman got out and went inside the house. She noticed that her father used a key from his keyring to let them in.

Perdita had drawn up a few cars behind the taxi. She stayed where she was, confident that neither her father nor the woman would notice her; they were too absorbed in each other. Another traffic warden was sauntering down the street, notebook in hand and Perdita moved the car forward past the house as a van that had been delivering stuff to another house drove away, leaving a convenient space. Perdita put the Audi in and sat there watching the house.

She waited a long time. Her mother would go ballistic waiting for her swatches but Perdita couldn't care less about that now. She's always *accusing* me of being incompetent so I bloody well will be, she muttered to herself as she sat there staring at the pansies.

Children came home from school, shrieking, shouting, roaring their exuberance to the sky. Mothers gathered young families close and shepherded them indoors with talk of tea and TV. They hauled prams and strollers up steps, bright women in shirts and jeans, shining hair and good teeth. Their men would be home later, barristers, doctors, businessmen. Comfortable.

Perdita sat very still for a long time until, at last, Lucas emerged. He glanced to the right and the left, then turned and waved to a window upstairs. Perdita ducked down to see. It was the soft redhead and she was obviously *en déshabille*. A satin housecoat slid off one rounded shoulder and white marble breasts were almost revealed under gossamer lace. She looked wanton and infinitely desirable.

She waved back at Lucas and blew him a kiss. Lucas turned then and strode away.

Perdita sat there, uncertain what to do next, emotions churning within. She wanted to go, run away and hide, but also she wanted to stay, know the truth. Face the fear of what she would find out. What can of worms she was opening. But she knew too that she could not go back. It was too late for that.

A bunch of girls in school uniform sauntered down the street eating apples, chewing gum, shoving each other good humouredly. One of them, a redhead, came tripping down the street and, turning, ran up the steps, took a key from her pocket and let herself into the house Perdita's father had emerged from only a short time before.

Perdita waited for a while, then got out of the car. She crossed the road and went up the steps to the house, heart thumping. She looked at the bell but there was no name on it.

As she looked the door opened and the girl stood there. She had changed into tennis clothes: an aertex polo, white shorts, tennis shoes and socks. Her red hair was pushed off her forehead by a white bandeau. She was very like her mother.

'Hi,' she said, bright-eyed and helpful, 'Can I help you?'

'I'm looking for, for a person called ...' Perdita couldn't think, saw a van down the street with the name McLeish and something about Tree Experts printed on the side and she swiftly said, 'Tree. Mr Tree.'

The girl laughed and shook her red hair, 'Oh no! We're not Tree. We're Morrison.'

'I'm so sorry.'

'Not at all,' the girl frowned, 'And I don't think you'll find a family called Tree along here. Not that I've heard of, and we know most of our neighbours.'

'I'm sorry.'

'Don't apologise.' Then she called back into the house, 'Mom, we know anyone called Tree?' There was a reply but Perdita could not hear. 'Sure it's not Parson's Lane? Or—'

'No, no. I'll check. Thank you.' Perdita ran down the steps breathless suddenly. The girl closed the door behind herself as Perdita got into her car and she waved, and hurried down the road swinging her racket.

There was a paper shop just around the corner beside a pub and Perdita went in and bought a paper. There was no one in the shop except an aged Pakistani woman who was serving. She sat on a stool behind the counter fiddling with her sari, obviously bored. Perdita guessed this was a slack time for her, just after the schools had decanted the sweet-loving hordes and before the commuters returned home, popping in for fags and the newspaper.

'You know a family called Morrison?' she asked the woman.

She nodded. 'Yes,' she said, 'we deliver papers. *Times* readers. And the *Independent. Vanity Fair*. Number sixty-seven. Very nice family.' She shook her head. 'Never see the husband though. It's not good. A man is the centre of a family. How can you call it a family without the head?' she appealed to Perdita, who shrugged. 'You *can't!*' she said with finality. 'People don't understand. If the man is not in charge all discipline vanishes. Society goes to the bad when you disturb the balance.' This was obviously her favourite topic and Perdita wondered what her children had done to warrant her strong feelings.

'So it's Mrs Morrison and her daughter?' Perdita hazarded.

The woman frowned, 'Oh, Mr Morrison is *there*. But not the *head*. It's wrong, don't you think? A woman controlling!'

It must be her daughter-in-law, Perdita decided, upsetting the balance for the woman. 'The head of *that* house is Mrs Fern Morrison. She has a daughter Miranda and a son, David.'

'Oh, she has a son too?'

'Sure. He is animal doctor. Though why people want doctors for their animals I dunno. Silly.'

'A vet?'

'Yes that's it. A vet. National Health is in a mess. They need doctors, but he does *animals*.' She clicked her teeth disapprovingly. 'They have a practice down the King's Road. Not far.' She looked curiously at Perdita. 'Why you want to know?'

'Oh, just . . . are those the strongest mints you have?' she asked changing the subject.

'No, no, these are best.' Perdita paid for them and left.

She was too far gone now to turn back. She wondered about Mr Morrison who was there and not there. She left her car where it was and

64

walked to the King's Road, went up and down both sides of a couple of blocks and eventually found 'Morrison & Burton Veterinary Surgeons' on a brass plaque.

The entrance was smart; modern chairs that looked comfortable, a glass table in the centre piled with magazines and a bowl of flowers. There were notices on the cork board on the wall; people searching for lost pets, puppy breeders advertising, litters of puppies or kittens available with the stricture, *An Animal is for Life. Scooby Don't: a Frisky Dog means Unplanned Puppies. Have your dog neutered— the National Canine Defence League*. A sign said that David Morrison BVSc MRCVS Veterinary Surgeon and Laurence Burton BVSc MRCVS Veterinary Surgeon were the men to see if there was anything wrong with your pet. 'Don't leave it until it is too late,' you were warned.

A tall, red-haired young man came out of another room as Perdita spoke to the receptionist who sat behind a small partition where files were obviously kept.

The young man spoke as she opened her mouth. 'Can I help you?' he asked.

'Mr Delsey to see you, Mr Morrison. His Betsy is poorly.' The receptionist glared at Perdita and said loudly, 'If you could wait your turn.'

'All right, Rita,' David Morrison glanced towards a little man with a cat carrier on his knee. There were angry sounds coming from within the cage, spitting and hissing. 'Be with you in a mo,' he said to the little man, then to Perdita, 'Can I help you?' he said again.

The man with the spitting cat stood up and came towards the young red-haired man. 'My Betsy is poorly,' he announced, glaring at Perdita. 'I was next, Mr Morrison.'

David Morrison smiled at her. 'Can I help you?' he repeated, looking at her with admiration in his eyes. Then, 'Just a moment, Mr Delsey, I'll be with you in an instant.'

Perdita shook her head. 'I'm afraid I'm a fraud. I came here to find out . . .' she faltered. Mr Delsey and Rita the receptionist were staring unblinkingly at her. Colour flooded her face.

'Mr Morrison! Mr Delsey's been waiting a long time . . .'

'I'd like to talk to you . . . talk to you . . .' Perdita stammered.

'Look,' he took her arm and led her to the door, 'I finish here in five minutes . . .' He grinned ruefully, 'or however long Mr Delsey's Betsy takes.' He was whispering. 'Maybe we could have a quick drink? There's a pub opposite. I'll see you there in five, ten minutes, okay?' She nodded and he raised his voice again. 'All right, Mr Delsey, come with me.'

She waited apprehensively in the pub. She ordered a lager and sat at a table in an alcove sipping it, picking absent-mindedly at a coaster advertising Guinness. There was a mock fire near her and it glowed redly. The pub was full of sunshine rays slanting onto the worn wood floor.

What would she say to him? She had no idea. She could not tell him the truth, could she? Your mother is sleeping with my father? In the name of heaven, what could she say? She nearly bolted, but something held her back.

He came into the pub, blocking the sunshine for a moment. There was a wonderful vitality about him and he went to the counter, ordered a beer and came and sat beside her. 'You like another?' he pointed to the lager. She shook her head. 'No, thank you.'

He was very like his sister; thick red hair brushed back, bright green eyes flecked with brown. Good skin.

'Now, how can I help you?' he asked. She blushed and lowered her head. He smiled. 'Oh Lord, it's not that bad, is it? What has happened? Your cat? Your dog? Passed away? Oh, don't look so upset,' he cried, obviously concerned.

She nearly lied and nodded. She *could* pretend her pet had died, but truth telling was deeply ingrained in her and she could not bring herself to play a game.

'I don't mean to be flippant,' he said.

'No, no. This is so awkward,' she felt ashamed of her prying, unable to think what to say.

'Well, no use beating about the bush. Spit it out!'

'Look, maybe I'd better go,' she stood up, 'I think I've made a mistake . . .'

He rose and pressed her firmly back into her seat. 'No. Tell me what this is all about. I'm a big boy, I can take it.' He grinned. 'Besides, I like looking at you. It's a long time since I've seen a girl as pretty . . .' he frowned, 'no. Beautiful,' he amended and leaned back, watching her.

'Well, you're going to hate me in a minute,' she said.

'Then don't tell me!' he said. 'I don't want to know. Let's just have this drink and enjoy ourselves.' He held out his hand. 'I'm David Morrison,' he said.

'Perdita Hastings.'

'What a lovely name. What do you do, Perdita Hastings?'

'My mother's an interior decorator. I work for her,' she clapped her hands against her cheeks. 'Oh gosh! She sent me to Colefax & Fowler ages ago to get stuff and I forgot. Oh help! She'll be furious!'

'Oh, I dare say she'll forgive you. Don't rush away. We've just met.'

'So here you are!'

Someone stood over them, blocking the light. She looked up into still grey eyes, the gentlest eyes she'd ever seen, calm and compelling.

'Ah, Larry! You finished? This is Perdita Hastings. Lovely name, isn't it?'

Perdita was caught in his glance, trapped there in those grey pools of warmth. She could not remove her gaze from his. 'Perdita this is Larry Burton, my colleague.'

He gave her a feeling of peace, of reassurance, a feeling that everything was going to be all right. She'd never experienced such a feeling before. She'd heard other girls in school say their daddies made them feel safe but she had no experience of it up to now, up to this moment.

Confused and near tears suddenly, she glanced from one to the other, feeling like an intruder in the midst of goodness, an alien there. If they knew what I am really like, she thought, why I had come. To shatter their peace, sow doubt and dissension. She shivered as the two men stared at her. She stood up and picking up her bag she fled leaving them gazing after her.

CHAPTER SIX

Her mother was furious with her, disproportionately angry. 'I can't trust you to do the simplest errand without you making a mess of it,' she cried. 'Where have you been? Where's the stuff I wanted?'

'I didn't go!' Perdita said defiantly, flinching as her mother glared at her.

'You didn't *go*? Where the hell *were* you then? You're gormless, you know that, Perdita? Sometimes I think you are mentally challenged. That's what they call it now, but where I come from we call it soft in the head. And it's too late now. The shop will be closed.'

'Let me zip over there, Melinda. I just might make it,' Posy was bright and eager. She glanced sympathetically at Perdita, then raised her eyes to heaven behind Melinda's back, and when Melinda turned and flipped her the car keys Perdita mouthed, 'thank you'. Posy caught them and was gone.

Melinda stared at her and raised one eyebrow, shaking her head slowly as if in bewilderment. 'Why can't you be more like Posy?' she asked in a tired voice. 'What did I ever do to deserve a child like you!'

Perdita didn't reply. She was used to it. She tried to let the things her mother said flow over her but they never failed to sting. Her head drooped. Melinda came nearer and pushed Perdita's shoulder-length hair back from her face.

'Your hair's a mess dear. You'll have to do something about it. Get it cut properly. Go to Nigel. He's a genius.'

Her mother's hair, the same colour as her own was cropped stylishly short. She fiddled with her daughter's hair a moment as if she had

70

every right to paw it. 'Oh leave me alone, Mother,' Perdita cried.

'Now, now dear, don't be pettish with me.' She wagged her finger under Perdita's nose. 'I'm seriously thinking of sacking you,' she said calmly, dropping the bombshell, 'so you be careful, my girl. One more day like today . . .' she shook her head again and moved away, 'and you are out!'

Perdita's heart sank. If her mother let her go she'd be jobless. Perdita didn't think she'd get another one, did not believe she was capable. There was so little she could do. She crept away as she often did, trying to avoid her mother's eyes. Melinda seemed to forget all about her when she was out of sight. It was when she was in her mother's presence that she was a constant irritant to her parent. So she slunk away.

*   *   *

Never in her whole life had Perdita managed to surprise her mother. Melinda was always so composed, in charge of things and, Perdita had to admit to herself, she was so predictable. Why would her mother be surprised at anything she could do?

The following day, however, Perdita had the unique pleasure of seeing her mother's composure totally wrecked. Melinda came to find Perdita, who was lurking behind a pile of

71

Peter Jones curtain material, and there was an expression of utter astonishment on her face. Gob-smacked was how Perdita described it to herself.

'It's for you,' she said in disbelief, 'the phone. A *man!*'

'Thank you, Mother.' Perdita, though inwardly excited, managed to look calm and unruffled.

Her eyes wide, Melinda glanced at Posy. 'Can you believe it?' she asked. She gaped at Perdita as she took the call.

It was David Morrison.

'Remember me?' he asked, 'the fellow you ran out on yesterday?'

Melinda was standing right beside her, staring in amazement at her daughter.

'Hi, David. Yes, I remember.'

'I got your name out of the book. Phoned you at home and got your message there that you were at work. You told me you worked with your mother, so it wasn't difficult.' She could tell he was smiling. 'Well, it struck me we had unfinished business.'

'What do you mean?'

'I mean, lovely one,' *Lovely one! Lovely one!* Perdita glanced at her mother. Melinda's blue eyes were boring into hers, puzzled, disbelieving. *Lovely one.* 'I mean, I'd like to get to know you better, Perdita.'

'But . . . but . . .'

'No. No buts. And don't sound alarmed. I'll

72

be civilized. I can't think why you treat me as if I were Jack the Ripper and I promise hand on heart I'm *not* the big bad wolf! I'll not gobble you up. So, here's what I suggest . . .'

'No, no I can't . . .'

'*Listen.* Let's meet in the pub we were in yesterday for a drink and a chat. I promise I won't pry. *Please*, Perdita. About six? How does that grab you?'

Looking at her mother's incredulous face, Perdita suddenly thought, why not?

'Okay. Fine,' she said.

'Good. And don't worry. You don't have to talk about anything you don't want to. Okay?'

'Sure. See you then.' She put the phone down. Her mother went on staring at her.

'A date?' she asked. Perdita nodded.

'Who with? The Elephant Man?'

Perdita did not answer. Posy was contemplating some huge over-sized Chinese vases. Melinda called to her. 'Hey, Posy, hear that? Perdita has a date!'

'Oh, jolly nice Perdy,' Posy sounded sarcastic.

'Why don't you go too, Posy? Just for a while. Tell us what he's like. Check he's not blind!' Her mother watched as Perdita's head snapped up. 'Oh no!' she cried in alarm, before she could stop herself.

'Only joking,' her mother's eyes narrowed. 'But it *might* be a good idea. You have no idea, Perdita, have you? You need protection.'

Perdita did as she usually did and slid away into the shadows hoping her mother would forget about her altogether.

*   *   *

Perdita slipped out of the office surreptitously, by the back way, at five-thirty. She would not put it past her mother to have Posy spy on her. She looked right and left, decided to shake anyone who might be following her and took the longest route to the Fulham Road.

It was fun, pretending she was shaking off a tail, doubling back on herself, jumping on the eleven bus to Hammersmith, catching the tube to Knightsbridge, then the twenty-two to the Kings Road and the thirty-one to the Chelsea and Westminster Hospital on the Fulham Road, then walking back to the pub.

By the time she got there she knew there was no way Posy or anyone, no matter how skilled, could still be tailing her.

She hoped what she was wearing would be all right. She always wore the same outfit, it was her uniform. Blue jeans, a white shirt, a navy cashmere cardigan and a navy blazer. Her mother had tried to put her into power suits but she categorically refused to wear the tiny clinging skirts and ornate jackets, saying she felt damned uncomfortable. Melinda told her that to look good that was how you were supposed to feel. Posy, however, had no such scruples and she often wore Melinda's cast-offs. Neat little multi-coloured Christian Lacroix outfits, Karl Lagerfeld designs.

'Anyone else would be grateful,' Melinda told her daughter. '*Posy* is grateful. But not you, Perdita. Oh no!'

She was late. David was waiting for her at the same table near the fire.

'Oh good,' he said when he saw her, 'I thought you'd shied away again. Stood me up.'

'No.'

'Sit down. What will you drink?'

'Lager please.'

She was sitting alone at the table in the gloom when Larry came in. He saw her and her heart stood still and she felt as if she was suffocating. All the breath seemed to leave her body and her chest felt as if it was held in a vice.

'Hello! You're the girl from yesterday, aren't you? Um . . .' he wrinkled his brow. 'Ah, Perdita, isn't it?'

She nodded. She couldn't speak. David returned with the drinks and when he saw his partner his face fell.

'Christ, Larry . . . don't tell me I'm wanted!'

'Sorry. Sorry old boy,' Larry held his hands up in a gesture of surrender, 'emergency! Mrs Nelson needs you. She says Prissy's had a bad turn. She said she tried to bleep you but . . .'

'That's because I turned the damn thing off. Because, guess what? I didn't want to be disturbed,' David said crossly.

'Well, she called the surgery. Said you'd promised you would come when she called. No one else will do. Prissy is in pain.' He turned to Perdita. 'She has no one else in her life. She loves that animal like a child.'

'Oh, damn Prissy!' David put Perdita's drink down in front of her. 'Okay, okay. I'll go. Sorry Perdita. I *did* promise. Will you wait?'

'I'll keep Perdita company,' Larry smiled at her and she smiled back. His smile enfolded her like a warm blanket on a cold day.

David left. 'He likes you,' Larry said, then leaning forward, 'problem is . . . so do I.'

'You didn't . . .?' She knew he hadn't set it up; he simply wasn't the type.

'Oh no!' he sounded shocked, 'I wouldn't do that.' Then he smiled again. 'Not that I wouldn't be tempted. But David is my friend and partner and I wouldn't do anything . . . Mrs Nelson is kosher. Scout's honour,' he glanced away into the fire. 'But I could have sent Rita, our receptionist to deliver the message to David. But,' he smiled at her again 'I wanted to see you. See if you had the same effect on me.'

'What effect?' How stupid I am to ask him that. I suppose I should know, she thought. But how could she know? The experience was totally new to her.

'Well,' he leaned across the table, 'when I see you my heart leaps into my throat. Like it used to do when I was a kid and the headmaster sent for me. I feel I might choke. It's not entirely pleasant.' His expression was rueful. Was he making fun of her? 'I have difficulty breathing,' he added.

'Oh I *know*!' It was out before she could stop herself. It was naïve, she knew that but it seemed she had lost all reservation. That sturdy barrier she had so carefully built around herself, that wall she had erected between herself and the world seemed to have tumbled down like the walls of Jericho.

'You felt it too? Oh good. That settles that!' He sounded very businesslike. 'Then I think you should tell David before he gets too interested. He is, you know. He's gone on and on about you and we can't see each other unless we are both up-front with him.'

'Is that necessary?' she asked, not relishing the idea at all.

'Well, don't you see, once you started going out with him I wouldn't try to take you from him. It wouldn't be fair.'

The idea of telling David anything at all appalled her. What would she, could she say? I'm interested in Larry not you? No. She would never be able to drum up enough courage to tell him that out of the blue. She had always found it impossible to be that straight with people, afraid she might hurt them as her parents hurt her.

'I can't,' she said helplessly, twisting her fingers together.

She looked so distressed that Larry found

the impulse to console her irresistible. He leaned forward and in the same gesture her mother had used, but oh so tenderly, he pushed the hair from her face. 'Then I will,' he told her. 'Hey, it's not the end of the world. You haven't said you'd marry him or anything.'

'Oh gosh, no!' Her eyes were huge pools of misery and he wondered who had managed to bruise her spirit so dreadfully. She was like the wounded animals he treated. She wrenched at his heart, touching him deeply and he wanted to ease the pain of her mute pleading.

'I'm very stupid,' she told him. 'You don't know how stupid I am.'

'Don't ever say that again,' he commanded seriously, his voice tinged with anger, 'never, do you hear? You are certainly *not* stupid. What gave you that idea?'

'My mother is always telling me. And she's right.'

He shook his head. 'No she's not,' he contradicted her firmly. 'And what does your father have to say about it?'

She sighed. 'Oh, he thinks so too. He agrees with her. It's about the only thing they *do* agree about. So you see . . .'

'I think *they* are the stupid ones.'

'Oh no! My father is *very* clever. Everyone knows that.'

'We had a saying in school Perdita, a silly childish taunt. But I've discovered it is true. When anyone teased us, calling us names, we'd

78

shout back, you know, the way kids do, "What you say is what you are!"'

'But my father is a brilliant man. You must have heard of him, Lucas Hastings?' His eyes narrowed. 'Now, you see! You're shocked. He's a political commentator, a brilliant journalist. Everyone who knows me cannot believe I'm his daughter. He thinks I'm dumb. And Mother! She's so bright. So clever. Compared to them I'm a total slouch. They are both so successful.'

'I didn't say they weren't successful. Or clever. I said they were stupid. You can be clever and stupid at the same time, you know. Clever at political commentary, at maths or physics, world affairs, facts, figures, everything, *but* stupid about human emotion, about feelings. About people. Your parents, Perdita, may be brilliant but they are utterly stupid about you.'

'How do you know?' she asked wondering about how sure he was.

'It's obvious!' he said. 'Now, that's all I have to say on the subject.'

There had been few people around but now the pub was becoming crowded. Perdita did not mind. Truth to tell she did not notice. It seemed to her she was alone in the whole wide world with this wonderful person, the two of them the only people there. Isolated by their awareness of each other. His smile enchanted her, put a spell on her. She smiled back at him creating a warm intimacy between them.

79

'Now,' he said. 'From now on you are not to worry about *anything*. I'll talk to David and you and I will have dinner tomorrow evening after I've had a word with him. Okay?' She nodded. If he had asked her to go to Abu Dhabi on the morrow she would have happily obeyed.

'Will David mind?' She hated so much to displease anyone, hated anyone to think she had behaved badly.

Larry smiled sadly. 'I guess he will,' he answered. 'I don't think he'll be at all pleased. After all, you are his discovery. But,' he spread his hands, 'thank God it's not a question of first come first served, Perdita. It won't kill him. Anyhow,' he added briskly, 'you cannot go out with someone when you fancy someone else. It's not honest.'

'Is that what I feel? Fancying you?'

He looked at her and the expression in his eyes melted her heart. 'Yes. Oh yes, I hope so,' he breathed.

She rose. 'I'd better go,' she said.

'Yes. I'll call you tomorrow. What's your—'

'No. No, don't do that. I'll meet you here. Same time.'

He nodded. 'And Perdita,' she looked down into his clear eyes, 'don't believe what they tell you,' he told her, 'they are quite wrong.' His heart swelled painfully at her expression, her trembling lip, her disbelief. She had been so hurt and as she returned his gaze steadily there was trust and gratitude in her eyes.

'Thank you,' she whispered.

She left the pub on wings of joy. She felt as if she floated six inches above the ground. No one will spoil this for me, she decided. No one.

CHAPTER SEVEN

'So she's done another runner.' David plonked himself down in the chair Perdita had just vacated. 'What's the matter with the girl? I'm not gruesome, Larry, am I? Or are you simply not telling me that I'm really the Frankenstein monster?' David was laughing.

'She hasn't, David,' Larry said calmly.

'Hasn't what?'

'Done a runner.'

'Ladies?'

'Uh-uh!'

'Oh heck! She had someone else. That's it. She was meeting her boyfriend. And I really fell for her. Ah well! *C'est la vie!*'

'No, David. It's not that either.'

'Let me get a drink. I can't bear this.'

He fought his way to the counter, exchanging pleasantries with the barman, getting his beer. Larry sat waiting patiently, watching him, a worried frown creasing his brow.

When his friend returned he took a deep breath and said, 'David, I've something to tell

81

you and I don't think you are going to like it.'
He met David's enquiring look squarely,
cleared his throat and continued, 'Perdita and I
have clicked. *Wham*—like that! That's the
truth. Sorry.'

Davis blinked. 'But I . . . but we . . .'

'I don't know how or why it happened,
David, but it did.'

David glanced at his friend. 'Oh, thanks a
bunch! Since when have you descended to
stealing your best mate's girlfriend?'

'She wasn't your girlfriend. You just fancied
her. Well, she fancied me.'

Larry felt relieved. David's reaction was
irritated, slightly miffed, but certainly not
heart-broken. He did not seem deeply
resentful. Larry had been afraid that their
friendship might be at risk and that was
something he would not be happy about.

Larry valued their friendship. He was a loyal
person and he did not make friends lightly.
David had been his mate since university. They
had set up a practice together and worked and
travelled together peacefully ever since. They
rarely had a disagreement.

They had the same interests in animal
welfare, girls and Chelsea Football Club. Larry,
much as he was drawn to Perdita, would not, at
this point, have easily given up his friend for
her. If David had been really disturbed, Larry
decided, he would have backed off. If David
had been very upset he would have phoned

Perdita and, as unhappy as it would have made him, he would have cancelled their date on the morrow, swallowed his feelings about her and fled to Egypt until the pain subsided.

But David was all right about it and Larry smiled, relieved, and relaxed.

The two began to talk about Egypt and their work there with the animals. Larry was trying, without much success, to organise a fund-raising event in Lambourne, Berkshire where his mother lived. They discussed the pros and cons of a garden fête, a pop concert or a pet competition. As evening lengthened into night-time they decided that the best idea would be an amalgamation of all three. 'God, I wish we had a higher profile,' Larry said, and David nodded.

'We can't afford a PR person,' David said ruefully.

'Some day,' Larry sighed, 'Some day, mate.'

*   *   *

Five years earlier the two vets had taken a trip to Egypt, a holiday, simply to sightsee, look at the Pyramids, the sphynx, the King Tut relics in the museum in Cairo. They were hoping to enjoy themselves, but the trip turned out quite differently.

What had happened was to change their whole lives. They had been sucked into a quite unexpected relationship with Egypt, her animals, her people. They became involved more deeply than either of them could have imagined. Instead of simply sightseeing the pair got embroiled, quite by accident, with an animal welfare organisation, although their friend Yasser Assam insisted it was not really an accident but the will of Allah.

Be that as it may, on that first trip they were visiting a souk, buying presents for the folks at home when Larry drew in his breath and clutched David's arm.

In front of them in the crowded bazaar a man was beating his donkey with such force that he had drawn blood. The donkey shrank under the blows, shivering in pain. He seemed worn out, too ill-nourished to try to avoid the violence, too exhausted to rear up or otherwise physically protest. No one paid any attention except the two Englishmen.

Outraged Larry ripped the whip from the man's hands and the man screamed back at him. A crowd was collecting and David became worried that they might find themselves in serious trouble. Such interference from outsiders was not appreciated here in Cairo. But Larry, incensed, was oblivious to the hostility he was arousing.

'This animal is in a bad condition!' he told the screaming man. 'Not good. Sick.'

The narrow street was littered with rubbish. An old man with a brown face criss-crossed with lines like a walnut, sucked on a hooka just inside his stall. He was used to turmoil in the bazaar, the shouts of vendors, the arguments, the haggling. It was all the same to him.

The crowd was mainly Egyptian in their long robes and head-dresses. There seemed to be no other Europeans around and Larry and David were very much alone.

The crowd clustered around the two friends, hostility growing as the man with the whip screamed at them, saliva collecting at the corners of his mouth and, leaning over, tried to retrieve the whip from Larry.

'The donkey is sick. Sick.' Larry reiterated, undaunted, and quite furious. If there was anything guaranteed to anger Larry Burton it was the sight of the strong picking on the weak.

'He doesn't understand you.' A cultured voice behind them made them turn. 'It is his way.'

'Well, his way is wrong!' Larry insisted, white-lipped.

'Peace, peace, my friend. We are on the same side.'

The man who addressed them was an Egyptian. He wore Egyptian clothes, an ema over his head and worry beads threaded through his fingers. He was a small man with a good-humoured face and he was frowning.

'We are trying to teach them,' he said. 'Leave him be for the moment,' he instructed, 'it is no use here and now.' He indicated the crowd. Then he held out his hand. 'Let me explain. I am Yasser Assam and I run the Cooke Hospital for Sick Animals here in Cairo. Perhaps you have heard of us?' Larry and David shook their heads. 'No, can't say we have.' The man sighed. 'Ah well, some day. Some day I hope you will.'

Larry grasped the man's outstretched hand. 'I'm Larry Burton and this is David Morrison. We are veterinary surgeons from London.'

'Ah! That is why you stopped. Most tourists, when they see such a sight as this,' he indicated the poor donkey staggering between the shafts of the cart, 'they turn their heads away, condemn the whole Egyptian race without understanding the circumstances, the poverty, the ignorance. And they go home. Do nothing. Well, we are trying to improve the situation, here and in Jordan. As far as India the Cooke Hospital for Sick Animals is spreading and doing good work.'

'It is appalling,' Larry looked at the tottering animal, his eyes full of pity, 'it is no way to treat an animal.'

The Egyptian shrugged. 'The man is poor. The animal is his only means of support,' he explained. 'You have no idea in the West. You are protected from the cradle to the grave. You do not understand when it is a matter of life and death. Literally. How can you? Well-fed bodies say I would die before I could harm my pet. But you have never felt *real* hunger. You have never been in the situation that man is in. He takes his anger, his frustration, his fear out

86

on the animal because the donkey is his livelihood and it has let him down and the man is staring death in the face.'

The donkey fell suddenly, in harness, pulling the man down off the cart after him. They watched in horror as the owner of the donkey screamed, jumped up and began to kick the dying donkey, yelling invective, exhorting it to get up. Then, when it became obvious to him that the donkey was dead he burst into tears and loud lamentations, calling on Allah, wringing his hands, moaning and shouting and waving his fists in the air.

'He has lost his livelihood,' Yasser murmured and sighed. He looked at the two men beside him. 'Come and have a coffee with me.' He bowed to them, then indicated a coffee stall a little further into the souk. 'There is nothing we can do here.'

'What will he do now?' Larry asked. The Egyptian spread his hands. 'Starve, unless he has another animal, which is doubtful. He wouldn't have been so violent with that one if he had.'

'But Mr Assam . . .'

'Call me Yasser.'

'Yasser. If the donkey was his only means of livelihood, then why did he beat it so?'

'Oh, to urge it on. To make it do the impossible. Make it young again. Fear makes him behave violently.' He strolled through the bazaar, nodding to right and left, returning greetings, leading them to the coffee stall. 'When the donkey or the pony, or ass or cow or whatever animal becomes old or lame or simply gets sick, they cannot *afford* either to release them for treatment or replace them. So they work them on and on, trying desperately to keep them going.'

'But it should never happen. The animals need care,' David said. 'They have the wrong end of the stick.'

'Do you think I don't know that?' The Egyptian's face was downcast. 'It is a sad business,' he said, then he brightened. 'Perhaps you might be able to help us,' he said, 'perhaps Allah sent you here to the bazaar today for just that purpose. Here. Good morning, Amar. Sit here.'

David and Larry sat on the small stools and sipped the thick black coffee out of tiny demitasse cups. People nodded and smiled at them now in the company of this man who was one of themselves, accepting the foreigners because Yasser had accepted them.

The Egyptians, David and Larry were to discover, were a good-natured people. Yasser told them all about his work with the Cooke Hospital in Cairo.

'It was an English lady who began it in the Twenties,' he told them. 'She was, like yourselves, outraged when she saw a similar sight as you did today, and she saw how the animals suffered. As I said, these people are poor. Desperately poor. There are no soup kitchens here, nowhere to go if you have no food, no Welfare State. Their animals are often their only means of support, their only means of transport, only means of income. Everything. They cannot afford to let them recover, give them the time and they are often kept working when they have crippling wounds, diseases or injuries. What we do, what the Cooke Hospital does, we provide free help and care for the maintenance and health of the animals.' He was leaning towards the two vets, speaking earnestly. They could see how passionately he felt.

'We provide free treatment and, in the case where the animal is worn out and there is nothing more we can do, we put it down humanely and give the owner a small subsistence allowance while they are without their means of livelihood, and until the owner gets from us a contribution towards another beast of burden.' He paused, then smiled at them. 'Oh, how I hate that phrase,' he said, shaking his head. 'If the animal is in no pain we let it have a few peaceful days before we put it down, probably the only proper rest it has had in years.'

Larry and David were moved. Yasser told them that the Cooke Hospital needed more help, more funds from the West to continue their work.

'We'll be glad to help,' Larry told him

impulsively, 'won't we, David?'

His friend nodded emphatically. 'Just let us know what to do, how best we can serve.'

'Information and education. We need friends to pass on the message,' Yasser told them. 'Now you must come and see the hospital and, if you would do me the honour, please dine with me tonight.'

They eagerly accepted the invitation. It was a productive meeting and they cemented a friendship. They kept in touch, participated, at first in small ways, then they became more and more involved in the life of the animal hospitals that spread across Egypt and Jordan. They raised funds for the cause, and at every available opportunity they helped out in the Middle East.

It became an obsession with Larry. It was his main interest. He only worked in the small practice off the King's Road in order to be able to afford to go to Egypt. He often flew to Cairo, Aswan or Luxor for the weekend to look in on the hospitals, give some practical help, dine with Yasser whenever possible and discuss ways and means to improve the situation. He gave lectures in Egypt and Jordan. And in London. The lectures helped enlighten people everywhere about the situation.

He discovered to his horror the full extent of the unconscious cruelty meted out to these overworked beasts, how they often laboured hour after hour in temperatures well over one hundred degrees Fahrenheit, with little opportunity of water or a rest in the shade.

As a Westerner he was appalled at the conditions prevalent in the Middle East, conditions inconceivable to people at home in Europe.

'What I cannot emphasise enough,' Yasser told Larry, 'is our *educational* work. We tell the owners, as you have seen, advise them on the future care of their animals which is after all in their own best interests.'

Larry and David were both heavily involved in the cause, but with Larry it became a passion. Inspired by all he had seen he became more and more interested and began to want to spend as much time as was humanly possible in Egypt.

He loved Egypt, its ancient culture, the sweetness of the people, their generosity and good humour. The place, the task, the Egyptians, became part of his life, perhaps the most rewarding and important part.

CHAPTER EIGHT

Next evening Larry and Perdita had dinner in La Famiglia at the bottom of the King's Road. Although the food was superb: Tagliatelle Ortolano, salad, baked swordfish, followed by a fabulous chocolate mousse and coffee, they did not do the meal justice.

If they did not eat much they did not speak much either. They sat opposite each other, oblivious to the chattering diners around them, the Italian *dolce vita*, the laughter, and examined each other's faces intently, eyes travelling over every inch, like small caresses. Larry discovered a tiny mole near Perdita's right eyebrow and saw that her golden hair was platinum near her pretty ears.

Perdita's eyes roamed lovingly over the lines on his sun-tanned forehead and at the corners of his grey eyes. They both knew there would be time for talk, time for laughter, time to eat. It was not necessary yet.

Afterwards, they strolled up the King's Road together. Larry took her hand in his and she shivered with pleasure. His hand felt rough and strong, the palm velvety-soft against hers. She had never felt so secure in her life before.

They took their time getting to know each other. They both felt their relationship was too important to rush. They went to the theatre together, and to concerts in the Albert Hall and the South Bank. They spent every evening in each other's company and Perdita, with passionate intensity, evaded her parents and Posy. She wanted to put off the inevitable meetings for as long as possible.

Larry brought her to meet his mother. His father had died of cancer when he was in his teens. 'That brought me and David close,' he told her. 'His father has multiple sclerosis, you see and is very sick. Has been for years.' The man of the house who was there, but not there . . .

When Larry's father had died his mother had bought a smallholding in the country, leaving, she said, the hubbub of London for the peace and serenity she found there. Her efforts had produced a wonderfully welcoming home, a delightfully old-fashioned cottage garden, an apple orchard at the back of the cottage beside a small running brook. It was picturesque and Anjelica Burton made no bones about enjoying her quiet existence buried deep in Berkshire.

Perdita was instantly drawn to her. She responded to the warmth and kindness she found in Larry's mother, the gentleness, the absence of the cruelty she was used to in her own home, the indifference she had seen in Posy's parents. She spent every weekend she could with Anjelica and Larry, getting to know them, basking and relaxing in their undemanding and uncritical acceptance of her.

The month of April came and went and on the last weekend in Meadow Cottage Larry kissed Perdita for the first time.

They were standing on the hump-backed bridge over the bubbling little stream, staring down at the dancing wavelets. The sun was cowslip-yellow and the air perfumed with the scent of honeysuckle and hawthorn.

'It's perfect here, Larry. Like something out

of an impossibly romantic movie,' she said.

Larry turned to her and, taking her face between his hands, he leaned towards her and kissed her.

Perdita let the bunch of wild flowers she held in her hands drop and drew in her breath as his lips met hers. A shock like an electric current coursed through her. Her body melted then, as his arms circled her, she almost fell at the sweetness of it, overwhelmed by a longing to melt completely into him, become part of him. He held her against him, supporting her.

'I love you, Larry,' she whispered as she raised a painfully exposed face to him, a face full of trust and hope and love, a face that reminded him yet again of the wounded animals that came to him to be healed.

'I know, my dear, I know,' was what he said, smoothing her hair from her brow.

They held each other tenderly. They were not in any hurry. Passion could wait. Larry was not about to hustle Perdita. He understood her modesty, her need to grow slowly into love, and Perdita, shyly and tentatively allowed Larry to know her, but slowly, little by little. For the first time in her life she began to put her trust into someone else, completely, without reservation.

'When will I meet your parents?' he asked her. 'It is usual, you know.'

She drew away from him and he could see her fright.

'Soon. Soon,' she said, turning her face so

94

that he could not see her expression, could not meet her eyes. She stared down at a black swan sailing serenely on the water. And remembered her father's words: *You're the ugly duckling who does not turn into a swan!* And she shivered.

'Perdita, you must not be frightened. You must trust me.'

'Oh I do. I do. But I don't trust *them.*'

'They can't hurt you now,' he protested.

She shook her head then turned to him. 'You don't know them, Larry, what they are capable of. You have never been exposed to … to cruelty.'

'My father died. That was cruel.'

'Yes, but he was a kind man. And your mother is an angel. No, I mean the cruelty of *people*, not the cruelty of fate. You cannot imagine or understand what it is like.'

'It can't be as bad as you make it sound, Perdita,' Larry insisted, not understanding. 'They can't hurt you if you don't let them. You're a big girl now. And I love you. Nothing can change that.'

She said nothing. She did not tell him that old habits die hard. She did not try to explain that verbal abuse cows one, that you learn to duck, to avoid, but never to assert your rights. The price you had to pay was too high and, anyhow, her spirit was too bruised to be able to do that. And her family had been playing the game too long for her protest to be listened to or be taken seriously.

She wished with all her heart that she could avoid introducing her parents to Larry. It would be wonderful if they never met at all and she could keep her relationship with him a precious thing apart, away from their soiling fingers. But she was a realist and knew this was a vain hope, she would eventually have to face the music.

CHAPTER NINE

At the end of that April she met Fern Morrison. It was unexpected, and unplanned. She had no desire to meet her father's lover and she had avoided David as much as she could without arousing either of the friends' suspicions. They decided she kept out of David's way because she was sensitive to his feeling of disappointment because she cared for Larry and because she did not want to cause a rift between the friends. This was partly true, though her self-esteem was never very great and did not allow her to feel that important.

Larry wanted her all to himself and this was easy to manage because when he was on duty David was off and vice versa. So they did not tend to clash. All three of them worked hard not to get in each other's way.

However, one glorious day Perdita popped into the surgery to pick Larry up and found he had been called out on an emergency.

'We're shutting up shop here,' David told her. 'Larry said he'd pick you up at my place in about an hour. We couldn't, off-hand, think of anywhere else you might comfortably wait for him.' He grinned at her. 'I won't try to seduce you, I promise,' he teased her, 'though I have to admit, I'd like to.' Perdita lowered her head, embarrassed. It was her own fault Larry knew she felt self-conscious sitting alone in public places. He had teased her about it, but gently, tenderly.

'They stare,' she said defensively, 'probably thinking how awful I am, that I'm alone because no one wants to be with me.'

'No. They are thinking how beautiful you are and they are probably wondering how they could meet you,' he told her, and she blushed and smiled.

She went home with David. He drove her.

'Great, there's a place to park right outside,' he said, easing the car smoothly in between a Jaguar and a Beetle. 'You bring me luck, Perdita. There's almost never a space here.' He cut the engine and looked across at her, his arm draped over the steering wheel. 'Remember the day I went to see Prissy? The day Larry stole you away from me . . .'

'Oh no he didn't!' she protested, 'He—'

'No. I know,' he smiled, shame-faced. 'That was unfair of me. But you remember that day? When I had to leave?' he asked again. She nodded. 'Well, Prissy's owner was so grateful for what I did,' he glanced at her sideways, 'and I assure you it was nothing; Prissy had a bone in her throat and I . . .' he made a chopping motion with his hand. 'It popped out,' he said, then, glancing away, 'She's written a cheque for the Cooke Hospital. A very large cheque. Larry has told you about the hospital and our involvement in it.'

'Yes, yes,' she cried. 'He talks about it all the time. He wants to take me there.'

'Well, so you see, you bring me luck,' he said, 'even if you don't love me.'

She shook her head, 'No,' she said, 'I don't, David. But I like you *so* much!' Then, hesitantly, 'You don't mind, do you? About Larry and me?'

He stared at her for a moment, then nodded. 'Yes I do,' he said, then more firmly, 'of course I do. You are the most beautiful—'

'I'm *not* beautiful!' she contradicted him, but felt a thrill of pleasure at the compliment just the same. 'I may be to Larry because he loves me,' she continued haltingly, 'but I'm *not* . . .'

'Yes you are! You don't know, do you? You have no idea. You, Perdita, are *truly* beautiful. Like Ingrid Bergman was. You are not manufactured, mass-produced, a clone, a copy. You are completely naturally beautiful. You haven't had your hair coloured, your body is not starved and your nose is not bobbed . . .'

'Should I get it bobbed?' she began, and he

98

shook his head angrily in contradiction.

'No, no, no, don't you *see*?' then he saw her face and realised she was teasing him, laughing to herself. 'No, listen Perdita. I mean what I say. If ever you break with Larry . . .' He heard her gasp and an expression of consternation crossed her face. '*If* it doesn't work out for you two,' he frowned, 'Larry is so . . . so tied up in the Egypt thing. I mean . . . he's a very self-contained man, he isolates . . .' he faltered to a stop, seeing her expression was aghast. 'Or maybe you just need a friend. Remember,' he imitated Humphry Bogart, 'you just have to whistle.'

She smiled at him. 'Thank you,' she said.

He leaned over and kissed her cheek. 'Thank *you*,' he said, then moved to get out of the car. Perdita glanced up at that moment and saw the woman there. Fern Morrison stood in the same window as she had stood that day when Perdita watched Lucas walk away from the house. She stood in the same pose, looking down on them and Perdita knew she had seen her son kiss her. And because she had been conditioned to feel fear, she was frightened.

CHAPTER TEN

Fern came into the comfortable drawing room moments after David had settled Perdita on the sofa. The room was large and bright, and very comfortable. The sofa was old and sagged, covered, like the armchairs, in flowered chintz. There were bowls of flowers everywhere and French windows led out onto a paved patio, a walled garden full of cherry blossom, magnolias, camellias and lilac. There was wrought-iron garden furniture, brilliantly white with a striped green and white umbrella over the table. There was a jug of lemonade and glasses on the table. David went and poured some for both of them and as Perdita put the glass to her lips the door opened and David's mother came in.

She was unfashionably plump, but trim, deep-bosomed with a small waist. Her skin was alabaster white and her legs were long and shapely. She had been in a *robe-de-chambre* at the window but had obviously pulled on the long floral skirt and loose white cotton knit. Her red hair shone like a burnished halo about her head and she seemed very nervous, very tense.

'This is Perdita Hastings, Mother,' David said, drinking his lemonade. His eyes were admiring as he looked at Perdita.

The woman frowned and her large green eyes were troubled. She had a voluptuous, pre-Raphaelite look about her that struck Perdita as very sexy and she thought how unlike Melinda she was. She also thought, she knows who I am and she does not like me being with her son, but what can she do? Perdita wanted to tell her not to worry, that she was Larry's girlfriend, not David's, but she didn't know how.

'I'm waiting for Larry, Mrs Morrison,' she managed and the woman smiled. She had small even teeth and her lips were very red but she wore no lipstick.

'Call me Fern,' she said, then stood with her back to them, looking out where the cherry blossom drifted like confetti over the small garden.

It was then that Perdita noticed the wheelchair half in and half out of an arbour at the bottom of the garden. She could just see the outline of legs under a tartan rug, two feet in hand-made leather loafers resting on a footrest. The arbour was draped in wistaria and the heavy clusters of mauve blossom hid the rest of the chair. It was obviously Mr Morrison, Perdita decided and wondered whether she would meet him. There was something faintly sinister about that chair, half-visible, protruding from the wistaria.

'Would you like a drink, Mother?' David asked.

Fern shook her head. 'No, dear.' Then, cocking her head, 'Ah, here's Miranda.'

There had been no sound, no warning, but moments later Perdita heard a clatter at the door and a girl's voice called, 'Hello Ma! Hi, you home?'

'In here, dear,' Fern called. David smiled at

Perdita.

'Mother's radar,' he said. 'She always knows when we're home before we get here.'

Perdita thought, that must be handy when my father is here. Jolly handy. Then she chided herself for being bitchy. She wondered, nevertheless, whether the man in the wheelchair waited there in the arbour while Lucas was visiting Fern.

Fern turned around as the girl who had opened the door to Perdita when she had first come to the house exploded into the room and threw herself at her mother, hugging her. Then, turning to David, she said, 'Can you help me with my bike, Dave? The chain's gone funny.' Then she noticed Perdita and she frowned, looking very like her mother.

'Hello! I've seen you before, haven't I?'

'No you haven't, brat,' David said, laughing. 'This is Perdita Hastings. My terrible sister Miranda.'

'Yes I have. I remember,' the girl was not going to be stopped.

'When?' Fern looked intently from Perdita to her daughter and back again. Perdita felt the blood rush to her cheeks. How could she explain what she had been doing at the door of their house?

'You rang the bell. Looking for someone called Tree,' the girl said brightly, 'last month. I thought it was a funny name at the time.' Fern was watching Perdita, hawk-like.

102

'Like Max Beerbohm Tree. Sir Henry Tree. No, it's quite common.' David was obviously puzzled and kept glancing from Miranda to Perdita and back, but he was trying too to be polite and charming and not upset Perdita.

The girl was sure of herself. 'Oh yes, I remember you,' she said, 'I remember thinking how beautiful you were. I'm a painter you see. I look at people's faces. I register them.'

'My sister, Perdita, is at *school*. She *hopes* to become a painter. But she has not yet.'

'I am what I am, now. I was born a painter and will always be a painter, Dave. Don't show your ignorance. Artists are born not made.'

'What is she talking about, Perdita?' David asked.

Perdita was saved by Fern. There was something in her eyes that told Perdita that she knew everything. She had guessed that Perdita had followed her father here and she did not want her children to know about any of this.

'David, go and see if you can fix Miranda's bicycle, there's a dear,' she said firmly. 'Your friend and I will sit a while in the garden and chat. Off you go.' She shooed them out of the room, giving them no opportunity to disobey, then she shepherded Perdita into the small garden, indicating the wrought-iron chair as she spoke. 'Sit there, do. There's a cushion. That's better.' She settled Perdita in the chair, 'It is nice here, don't you think? I know it's small but it's very pretty. The rhododendrons will be in bloom soon. They are a brilliant cerise and beside the white camellias and the mauve lilac they look wonderful.'

Perdita could tell she was chattering on, deciding what she would say. Then she remarked, 'Excuse me a moment,' and she went down the small paved pathway to the arbour. Perdita saw her lean over the wheelchair, her head and shoulders disappearing behind the wistaria. She could hear the murmur of voices, one dark, one light, but she was too far off to hear what they said. Then Fern tucked the rug in around the knees and Perdita could see a hand, thin, tapered fingers plucking at the checked material.

Fern returned and sat opposite her visitor. She glanced obliquely at her. 'My husband,' she said and Perdita saw her large green eyes were full of pain. 'He's an invalid. Very sick.'

'I'm sorry.' Perdita did not know what else to say.

'Why did you come here?' Fern asked gently. 'I saw you too, that day Miranda mentioned. You rang our bell and asked for a family called Tree? Why did you do that?' Perdita remained silent. 'Now you come here as David's friend. He has spoken of you a lot over the last weeks. So unlike him. He has never spoken so much about any girl before.'

'Oh, it's not David,' Perdita bumbled, 'it's Larry Burton. I'm . . . em, his girl-friend.'

'But David *is* interested in you, though? Am

104

I right?'

Perdita nodded. 'But I've *told* you,' she protested, 'It's Larry I'm . . .'

Fern Morrison waved an elegant white hand for silence. She leaned forward, putting her elbows on the white iron table. 'You followed your father here that day, didn't you?' she asked calmly. She had narrowed her eyes against the pale sunshine.

Perdita nodded. 'Yes,' she admitted reluctantly, 'I saw you come out of the restaurant that day. Mother sent me to Colefax & Fowler . . .'

'So you thought . . . what? I'm curious to know.'

'That you were his . . .' she could not think what to call her without sounding coarse and bitchy.

'Mistress?' Perdita nodded. 'Why not his quick lay? His tart? It could have been a thing of the moment. Impulsive. Just for that afternoon.'

A cloud passed over the sun, casting Fern Morrison's face in shadow. 'No,' Perdita insisted. 'There was something about you both together that made me realise that you knew each other very well. You were familiar with each other. I could tell that. It was not the first time.'

Fern stared at Perdita. She thought for a moment, then sighed. 'It's difficult,' she said. 'I've agonised about this since the day I saw you

105

down there in the street. I knew you would come back. Then David began to rhapsodise about you. I was frightened. Very frightened.'

'But why? If my father chooses to have an affair with you, what's it got to do with me?' Perdita, although she could not blame her father for looking for love outside his home, could not keep the sarcasm out of her voice. 'If it *was* David, which it isn't, what has it to do with you and Father?'

Then suddenly she went cold, for before Fern Morrison spoke she knew exactly what she was going to say.

'Because Lucas Hastings is David's and Miranda's father too. That's why I'm frightened. And I'm trusting you, Perdita, to keep this a secret ...' She glanced at the arbour. 'My husband does not know. Must never know. And David must never know.' She squeezed her eyes together and her hands on the table were knotted in a fierce embrace. 'My poor Paul,' she whispered, staring down where the wheelchair protruded from the arbour. 'He thinks they are his. We tried, you see, after he became ill. Up to then we thought we had plenty of time. We tried and it was agony. And useless, but he *thinks*, he believes ...' She frowned. 'We were selfish, you see, deciding not to have children until later. Then Paul was struck down. I tried to conceive with him but it didn't work. Couldn't have. And Lucas, your father ... I got pregnant. At first I was terrified.

I thought of abortion. It was an outrageous thought for me. I wanted children desperately. Then I thought, Paul need not know. It made him so happy. He did not feel useless any more. I decided on the lie I live now.'

She turned and looked at Perdita. 'I don't expect you to understand. I love Paul, you see. I love the man he was. He was my childhood sweetheart, only he never had the time or the opportunity to grow up. His pain put a stop to that. Like all invalids he is fretful and irritable. Difficult. But I'll never desert him. He would die without me. The children. His home.' She turned away from Perdita. 'I love Lucas too. It is a quite different love. Passionate. And he loves me, Perdita, and I'm sorry if that hurts you.' She stood. 'Oh why did you have to follow us? Why couldn't you have left things as they were? But I suppose that is unrealistic. It was bound to happen sooner or later.' She shook her head sadly. 'I've been afraid, all these years.'

'Afraid?'

'Yes, terrified would be more accurate.'

'Of what?'

'Paul finding out. It would kill him. Some busybody discovering the liaison, Lucas and me and telling the press. Can you imagine their glee, the field day they would have? They don't exactly *love* your father, Perdita. He has been . . . em, *short* with them to put it mildly. They would make hay with a scandal about him.' She sat down again, looking pleadingly at Perdita. 'He think's he's above all that, that he is invincible. He is careless, pays no attention.'

Perdita could well believe it. Her father would court danger arrogantly. 'And if it all came out he'd be the first to suffer. And David and Miranda. Most of all my children. His children. We cannot hurt them. You can imagine how confused they'd be if they ever found out. Oh, it would be such a mess.'

Perdita stared at Fern's hands, her fingers lacing and interlacing, her knuckles white and red.

'I was young, you see, so young. Madly in love. Lucas was famous. He said he did not love Melinda, she would never give him a divorce. And I knew I would never divorce Paul.'

She was appealing to Perdita as if her life depended on it. Perdita supposed that, in a way, it actually did. She felt as if she was floating, as if she was up on a stage in a dramatic play. None of this was real. It was too theatrical. Yet she knew too that all of it *was* true.

'I was happy, Perdita, as well as being frightened. It was all pat. All perfect. Paul thought he had sired two healthy children. This gave him such solace. I was having a passionate affair with your father. I was, you might say, having my cake and eating it. Now that I'm older I know that I was wrong, that there's always a price to pay and the ones who pay most dearly are usually the innocent ones. David and Miranda. I know now that the truth will out, but please don't tell them, Perdita, please.' She glanced at Perdita. 'I've never had the courage to break it off. Give up Lucas. You know your father, Perdita. He would never let me. He's not an easy man. And I love him. I would never do anything that might upset him and he won't let me go.'

The door banged and there was the sound of laughter in the hall and David's and Miranda's voices raised in light-hearted banter. The figure at the bottom of the garden had not stirred.

Fern brushed at her skirt with nervous fingers. 'I hope you won't say anything, Perdita. I had to talk to you about it. I saw David kissing you in the car, you see. He's your half-brother. I had to say something.'

'I know. It's all right. I won't say anything,' Perdita said, her head in a whirl.

'You won't tell David. Promise me.' Fern's lip trembled. 'I couldn't bear to lose him and I would, if he knew.'

'I promise.'

David shouted, 'Just washing my hands, Mother. Won't be a mo.' Then he popped his head round the door. 'Larry's coming. His car just turned in off the King's Road. He'll be ages finding a parking space. Maybe you'd better go out to him, Perdita,' and he disappeared.

'May I phone you?' Fern asked. 'I'd like to meet you. Talk to you properly. Tell you about—'

'Yes. Yes please. I would appreciate that.'

'All right.' Fern seemed satisfied and she turned into the drawing room as Larry entered, followed by David.

'Ah, Larry, how nice to see you. You got a parking space, then?' and without waiting for a reply Fern added, 'Do have some lemonade, do. It's fresh.' She was again the gracious hostess, welcoming her guests, holding up her cheek for Larry to kiss.

Perdita realised that no one had introduced her to Paul Morrison. She supposed they did not think her important enough to make the effort. Or perhaps he did not like company. But he had been at the bottom of the garden all that time. Still, she thought there was something faintly rude about it and wondered again where he was when Lucas called.

Perdita sat there feeling shell-shocked. She stared down to where the wheelchair was statue-still, then she too held up her face for Larry to kiss. But inside she was reeling from this avalanche that had hit her. She was trying to come to terms with the fact that she had a whole other family that up to now she had been completely ignorant of.

CHAPTER ELEVEN

That night in bed Perdita tossed and turned, fought with the pillow, was nearly strangled by her sheets and eventually gave up all attempts to sleep. She tried to sort out the whole tangle in her mind but failed to reach acceptance and therefore peace.

David was about the same age as herself and that meant her father and Fern had been lovers when Melinda was pregnant with Perdita. For some reason Perdita felt this was unfair. Not playing the game. Fairness was important to Perdita. She was a very fair person and she had to admit that for her father *not* to have had someone extra curricular in his life would have been almost an impossibility. Ditto Fern. She assumed the other women in his life had been red herrings to distract from the real situation and she reflected now that, in the main, her father seemed to behave outrageously publicly and she had often wondered whether he ever saw any of these dolly-birds privately. She had doubted it.

Perdita had not thought too much about it, but she doubted very much whether her father and mother ever made love. She had never seen any evidence of it. They never slept near each other at Oak Wood Court and lived separately in London. She had fancied that, like all young people who could not conceive of their parents 'at it' as they used to say in school,

111

that her mother and father *must* have a sex life. But as she got older it became more and more obvious to her that Melinda and Lucas did not appear to. Apart from their obvious antipathy towards each other there was a lack of opportunity. A contrived lack of opportunity.

Since Perdita had fallen so passionately in love with Larry Burton she recognised physicality in others. It was easy to spot, that tactile response even between people who hated each other but still felt a sexual tug or were not entirely indifferent to each other. Lucas and Melinda seemed to their daughter supremely indifferent, uncomfortable even. It appeared as if they found each other distasteful. So it seemed to her naïve to suppose her father was leading a celibate life. And it was as unrealistic to imagine a woman as obviously ardent as Fern Morrison would give up sex for life because her husband was an invalid.

Eventually she slept. She had decided not to allow the puzzle of her parents and the Morrisons to interfere with her own happiness and her happiness was tied to Larry. What had any of them to do with him? Nothing. She did not have to tackle their motives, their complicated lives. She let it drop.

Larry spent the next week trying to persuade her to come to Egypt with him. He was scheduled to spend some time in Luxor at the end of May. He said he could not, would not, be separated from her.

'You've got to come with me, see what I do there. It's important.'

She, bemused by his need, touched to the core by her indispensibility, nevertheless hesitated. She had never been out of England. Her parents never thought to take her with them when they went abroad. However, Melinda had sorted out Perdita's passport, although she had no intention of taking her daughter anywhere. It was typical of her mother, but now Perdita was grateful.

It was natural that Perdita was a little scared at the prospect. Her love and trust was at war with a totally irrational fear. She fought it and love and trust won.

Fern phoned Perdita and suggested they have tea in the Savoy. Perdita was not at all sure she wanted to become involved with Fern Morrison. She had enough on her plate with the whole Egypt thing and Larry and she would have been happier to completely avoid the situation so fraught with emotion, but she had stumbled into it and she did not know how to extricate herself. So she agreed.

Perdita arrived first and waited awkwardly for David's mother to arrive. Fern wore a long skirt and a low-necked black top and gypsy earrings. Her red hair tumbled around her face, emphasising her pale skin. The waiters rushed to her assistance with great enthusiasm and Perdita could only reflect on the aura of sensuality Fern Morrison exuded. She sat on the sofa, indicating the armchair in front of her for Perdita, and Perdita nodded and obeyed. Fern waited in composed silence for the tea to arrive and poured without comment. Perdita found the silence unbearable and shifted in her chair restlessly.

When the waiter had brought the cake-rack with sandwiches, scones and finger cakes and they were both nibbling a cucumber sandwich and sipping their tea, Fern spoke at last.

'Well, Perdita, what do you think of me? Am I the woman you hate? Cruella de Vil? The Wicked Witch of the North? Or is it the East? I can never remember.' She waited. The pianist was playing songs from another era. 'The Nearness of You'.

Perdita shook her head. 'No. I don't hate you,' she said at last. 'I know I should. I think I must be an unnatural child, but you see I don't really like my father and I *hate* my mother. I expect I would hate you if I loved them, but I don't.' She stared defiantly at Fern who met her gaze levelly.

'Really? Why?' she asked calmly.

To Perdita's horror, tears sprang to her eyes. The enormity of her mother's contempt for her suddenly seemed overwhelming. 'She despises me. She thinks I'm useless. How can you love someone who doesn't care a rap for you?'

'Easily,' Fern said.

Perdita blinked rapidly and the tears slid

114

into the corners of her eyes then dropped onto her cheek and trembled there before sliding down to her chin. 'Anyhow,' she said, 'she's right. I guess she must have hated having a daughter like me.' She leaned forward putting her cup down on the silver tray. 'You see, they're so talented. My mother is *perfect*. Her body is, well, perfect . . .'

'Yes. Lucas says she's a clothes horse,' Fern muttered, but Perdita continued as if she had not heard.

'Everything about Mother is neat and glamorous and attended to. Never a hair astray, never a nail chipped.' She glanced down at her own broad hands, the nails filed across, plain, almost antiseptic. Then she looked back at Fern. 'Then there's her work. Every job she does is a success. Meticulous. That hotel she just did—everyone talks about it. Compared to her I'm talentless, stupid, clumsy and ugly. Or so she tells me.' Perdita's voice was not self-pitying, simply matter-of-fact.

'Does Larry think you are ugly?' Fern asked.

'No, but—'

'Does David?'

'No, but Mother's standards are very high.'

'Have you ever heard of jealousy?'

Perdita's eyes widened. 'You don't imagine . . . that would be ridiculous!'

'Why, Perdita? It's quite common, you know, for a mother to be envious of a young daughter. And Melinda is in love with a man who does not love her. That makes for bitterness. Why not, Perdita?'

All Perdita's pat answers, all her deductions were thrown into confusion. She gasped, 'Because ... I've just told you. She's perfect! And I'm ... why on earth would she be jealous of *me*?' she asked incredulously.

'You are young, Perdita, and very beautiful, no matter what you think, and she must be very lonely. And loveless. Listen, Perdita, for a moment.' A frown creased the smooth white brow. 'When I came here today I did not know how you felt about things, whether you ...' she shrugged, bit her lip and continued. 'What happened, long, long ago, warped your mother and reduced her life to a lie. She trapped Lucas into marriage and it did not work. I'm sure your mother thought it would. It was not her fault that she is the way she is. And she *is* jealous of you. Maybe she's not even aware of it but you are young, beautiful—oh yes you are. You have your whole life ahead of you and she is growing old and her whole life must appear a sham when she thinks about it. Loveless and so sad. She cannot change now. It's too late. She's made her bed so she must lie on it.' Fern gave a wan smile. 'Most of us do,' she said.

'What happened? To make her the way she is? You said ...'

'I'm not sure if I ought to tell you this, but, well ... Do you remember your grandfather, Perdita?'

116

'Gramps Jack? Mother's father? Oh yes. He was always nice to me. Gave me chocolates when he shouldn't.'

Fern nodded. 'Yep. That sounds like him. Buying you. He bought everyone.'

'Oh no! I'm sure . . .' But she wasn't. Not at all.

Grandfather Jack was always giving her things her mother did not approve of. Grandfather Jack treated her mother, Perdita suddenly realised now, exactly as Melinda treated *her*. Grandfather Jack ordered her mother about, ridiculed her, spoke contemptuously of everything she did and often reduced her to tears. But he had always been nice to Perdita, though it upset the little girl when he whispered, 'Whatever you do don't grow up like your mother!'

'Your grandfather was a very big wheel in the BBC,' Fern said.

'Mmm. I know.'

'What you may not know is, he threatened to scupper your father's career, and believe me he was quite capable of doing so, if he did not marry your mother.'

Perdita stared at her. This she had not known. Fern put a dollop of cream on her scone and topped it with a spoonful of blackberry jam. Melinda would be appalled at such indulgence.

'I was going out with your father at that time. He had finished with your mother. It had all

117

been on her side in any event. She adored him and pursued him relentlessly. He broke it off and started to date me. Then Melinda found out she was pregnant, and all hell broke loose.'

She bit into the scone, licked the cream off her lips and sighed. 'Unfortunately, your father always put his career before anyone or anything. You can guess the rest. Jack Armstrong, when he found out his darling daughter was with child, as he insisted on phrasing it, went ballistic. He said if Lucas didn't marry his daughter, make an honest woman of her he'd make sure Lucas never worked in the business again. He'd have him black-listed. And he could do it. Jack Armstrong was quite capable of doing it.' She smiled at Perdita, 'Your mother was delighted. She was madly in love with Lucas, and unfortunately Lucas was career-mad.' She wiped her lips with the napkin. She wore no lipstick yet her lips were red as berries. 'You must understand, Perdita, that things were very different then. Not that many people used condoms. Sexual health was not the issue it is today.' She shook her head. 'Even today, with all the publicity, the warnings, people still take risks. Imagine what it was like then.'

'So my father was forced to marry my mother?'

Fern nodded. 'He needn't have, of course, he could have married me and lost his career. But he was seduced by Daddy Jack's power.

118

Position. Marrying Melinda guaranteed a glittering career. He had immediate entry into the world of the high-flyers, the big names, the stars. He would inherit Oak Wood Court, have access to property, money and, most important, a father-in-law who could make or break him. Who could ruin him, make sure he never worked in his chosen field *or* who could push him forward, make him a household name. When I was going out with him, before he,' she glanced at Perdita, 'sold out,' she said wryly, 'he was very small potatoes. He was at the bottom of the ladder. After he married your mother he was propelled to the top. Yup! He betrayed himself. He loved me, but he wanted the power, the fame, the fortune. He paid a high price for it, Perdita. I've watched him grow bitter. I've watched him as he grew to hate his wife. I've watched him doubting his own success. He wonders constantly if he would have made it without Daddy Jack's ruthless pushing. He's a very unhappy man, your father.'

'Then why did you . . . do you . . .'

'I love him. Don't you know yet that love tolerates all kinds of stupidity? And I'm still waiting for him to leave your mother.' She lifted an eyebrow. 'Do you mind?'

'No. No. They would be much better apart,' Perdita said. 'And you? Paul?'

'Paul had been madly in love with me for years. We were children together. He asked me to marry him when your father married Melinda and I did.' She waved a pale hand. 'Oh, it sounds complicated now, but it seemed so simple then. I was angry. Lucas had married another woman. Paul asked me and I seized the opportunity. How could I know he already had MS?' she averted her face but Perdita could see the pain mirrored there. 'No one knew. I suppose it was my punishment,' she said sadly.

'And what . . .?'

'Lucas came back to me almost at once. He left her bed after the honeymoon and ran to me with open arms and pleading eyes. He cried in my arms that night, Perdita, and deep inside he has been crying ever since. That night, David was conceived and Paul was told he had MS. What a tangle.' She turned to Perdita. 'I hope I haven't shocked you?'

Perdita shook her head. 'No. You've made a lot I didn't understand clear,' she replied.

'You see, what eats into your father is the knowledge of his own venality. She was the big man's daughter, his road to fame and fortune, and I was the daughter of a shop-keeper. No contest. But he hates the fact that he betrayed both himself and me for mercenary rewards. He likes to think of himself as an idealist. He's been at war with himself since he married your mother.'

'How could you put up with it?' Perdita asked, 'take him back?'

'I told you. I love him. I can't *not*.'

'And David doesn't know who his father is?'

'No. We became very careful. Lucas became paranoid. No one must find out. Old Daddy Jack was watching all the time. After all he only died a few years ago. And people were very moral in those days. Not like now. I remember a religious broadcaster lost his job and was discredited forever because he had an extra-marital affair. So did the presenter of a children's programme. Scandal could finish you in those days. It's different now but Lucas is in the habit of secrecy. He says it gives spice to our relationship, but I think it is simply habit. And his fear of the inevitable emotional wrangles. Like when David and Miranda find out. *If* they find out. And you of course. But,' she sighed, 'I live in hope.'

'Why didn't he come clean when Grandpa Jack died?' Perdita asked.

'Well, habit, as I said. And,' Fern poured more tea, delicately using the strainer, 'Daddy Jack's will was clear and air-tight. If Lucas divorces your mother he forfeits all rights to the properties and the money.'

'But he hardly ever uses Oak Wood Court and he doesn't need the money.'

'It's fear, Perdita. Habit. He simply cannot trust. He visualises a catastrophic scenario. Totally unrealistic.' She tut-tutted, then continued, 'You see, he's never had to stand on his own two feet and realise he can survive. Hard times are wonderful teachers. When you

121

survive you know you have it in you, the strength. He does not know that. Cheating is silly. It takes away confidence forever. Men! Dear Lord!'

They talked as the waiters removed the linen from the low tables and set them up for drinks. Tea-time was over. It was coming up to cocktail time and bowls of nuts and appetisers replaced the cake-racks and silver condiments. The piano player was having a break and the chandeliers were lighting up as evening fell. Dinner was being set in the River Room beyond them.

They talked and Perdita wished that Fern had been her mother. They parted, promises exchanged on both sides.

Fern said, 'Don't blow your opportunities, Perdita. Seize whatever happiness you can. Don't waste your life like your mother and father have done. Time goes by so quickly and suddenly it is too late.'

Perdita thought about her words and decided that, after all, she would go to Egypt with Larry.

CHAPTER TWELVE

Before they went to Egypt, Larry insisted on meeting her parents. Lucas and Melinda behaved beautifully, thereby utterly confusing

Perdita. Obviously they had decided for some devious reason that they would be on their best behaviour and Perdita did not know whether it was a joint decision or one reached independently.

Oak Wood Court lay bathed in spring sunshine as they drove silently up the long drive lined with oak trees, heavy and dark overhead, leading to the elegant entrance to the mansion.

Lucas and Melinda stood at the top of the steps waiting for them, welcoming smiles on their faces. They looked, Perdita thought, like a couple in a movie and she muttered, 'Oh Jesus!' under her breath.

'Your parents?' Larry asked in disbelief. 'I thought you said . . .'

Graham was waiting to take the car and park it and as Larry pulled up and got out of the Honda he took the keys from him. Perdita realised that she had made Lucas and Melinda sound like characters from a Stephen King novel and here they stood, side by side, the perfect couple. They never fail to hurt me, she thought, and wondered if she was totally mad for thinking such weird thoughts. Had she really wanted her parents to shout at each other in front of their guest? No, of course not. But this way made her seem a liar.

'Darlings!' Melinda cried, oozing charm, 'welcome!'

Lucas smiled his famous smile and said,

looking deeply and sincerely into Larry's eyes, remembering his name, a trick he learned long ago, 'So nice to meet you, Larry. Come inside. I'm sure you'd like a drink after the drive.'

The house had a formal atmosphere that Melinda had done nothing to change since her father died. Old Jack Armstrong liked to frighten his subordinates, so the place was intimidating. Melinda saw no reason to decorate the place, keeping it as a sort of shrine to Jack's memory.

They had drinks in the library, a sombre room with leather chairs and a huge log fire burning and Lucas waxed eloquent about ecology, how careless the man in the street was with regard to his habitat. He's done his homework, Perdita decided, and was not at all sure she appreciated the fact.

'It is appalling how indifferent we are to the way we are destroying the planet we live on,' Lucas said, one beady eye on Larry. 'It's disgraceful. I see a future where the mountains will be grotesque piles of discarded black plastic bags, the sea will be a sewer and the food will all taste of cotton wool, and,' he paused, thinking, 'what's that song? *Put 'em in a tree museum*. Like that! All the forests will be cut down and man will drowning in breathlessness. We may even have to buy oxygen in shops. Go around wearing masks. Having to purchase the air we breathe.'

Perdita could see Larry warming to him. He

had fallen under that potent Lucas spell, just as she had feared. She could practically hear his brain ticking over; why did Perdita paint such a harsh picture? This guy is great. Feels just like I do. She wanted to shout out, 'It's an act! It's all a sham!' But she remained silent.

She could not understand why this upset her. Wasn't it better that Larry liked her parents than not? She supposed that she wanted Larry on her side, understanding her, her frustrations.

Melinda was flirting now with Larry, drawing him out about his work in Egypt and he was responding to her charm like a plant to the sun.

They had lunch in the long dining room. The conversation, mainly between Larry and Lucas, was slightly provocative. It was the sort of repartee that Lucas was famous for in his interviews and Larry was holding his own beautifully. Perdita felt left out. Soured, her conversation uninvited, she realised with clarity that Lucas was showing her up. He was revealing to Larry his daughter's ineptitude. Her silence appeared sulky, and she supposed it was, but to Larry she must look clumsy, dull and uninteresting.

How she remained seated at that table she never knew. She wanted to run and hide, to leave Berkshire and flee back to London while her mother and father sparkled and shone. She yearned desperately to put miles between her father and mother and Larry. She knew she was being unreasonable. She despised herself for her awkwardness, her dullness, but could think of no way to change matters. She sat silently till her father remarked, 'Are you all right, pet? You haven't said a word for hours!' Perdita nodded. He never called her *pet*.

Lucas smiled at Larry and winked, twirling the stem of his wineglass between strong fingers. 'Perdita's being sulky again. She's a shy one, our Perdita. But I'll say this for her,' he glanced at Larry, 'she's got good taste.'

Perdita blushed. She tried to think of something clever to say but could not.

It had begun to rain and they returned to the library to have their coffee, truffles and *petit fours*. The maid brought the tray and poured and served the coffee. She was handing Perdita the demitasse cup when the door burst open and Posy came hurtling in. Perdita glanced at her mother and saw the malice in Melinda's eyes. She's done this deliberately, she thought, and her heart sank.

Posy was wet and, with the exuberance of a puppy she shook herself in front of the fire. Keeping up a babble of chit-chat, she greeted Lucas, Melinda and Perdita and then stopped squarely in front of Larry and asked, 'And who is this lovely man?' As if she didn't know! Perdita felt her cheeks glow redly and she admonished herself yet again for her evil assumptions.

126

From Perdita's point of view the afternoon went from bad to worse, though it seemed that the rest of the party found the time spent together delightfully entertaining. Larry and Posy laughed a lot. Lucas was witty and Melinda charming. Only Perdita, it seemed, was excessively quiet.

When the time came to return to London, Posy asked ever so prettily if Larry could give her a lift. Larry said, of course, very graciously and appeared only too happy to oblige. Perdita, intensely irritated at the intrusion, for she had planned to try to make Larry understand about how her parents appeared to him and how they treated her when there was no company on the way back, had no choice but to acquiesce and make the best of it.

Posy contrived to jump in the front seat of Larry's car leaving Perdita to climb in the back. On the drive home after Larry had shaken hands with Lucas and Melinda with assurances and reassurances that they would 'do it' again soon, much good-will all round, with many goodbyes littering the air, Posy began a subtle flirtation with Larry right under Perdita's nose.

Larry, partly preoccupied with his driving answered in kind, laughing and joking with Posy and Perdita sank into sullen silence in the back, certain now that she was totally uncivilised. She hated the fact that she felt as she did, envied her mother's and Posy's ability and despised herself for being a nerd.

When they reached Perdita's flat she was further upset when, instead of Larry joining her and Posy getting a taxi to her flat the latter pleaded with Larry, 'Could you, would you give me a lift home, Larry? Please? Perdy won't mind, will you, Perdy?'

Perdita was too tired, too defeated to argue. Afterwards she wondered why she hadn't said she wanted to speak to Larry. She could have said, 'If you don't mind Posy I'll call a cab for you.' That would have been fine, but she simply did not have the heart. She hopped out of the car with a remark about being tired and having to make an early start, ran up the front steps and let herself into her apartment before Larry could reach her. She burst into tears as soon as she had closed the door behind her.

CHAPTER THIRTEEN

Posy spent most of her life feeling utterly frustrated. She could not understand why, when she got what she wanted, as she almost always did, she was not happy. Like resembling Perdita, like the job at The Design Factory, like meeting the Hastings, getting herself invited to Oak Wood Court. Before she achieved her purpose she was confident that when she got there it would be over the rainbow time. It never was.

She wanted Larry. She knew she had to pounce or he would slip away and she would become, to him, merely Perdita's friend.

Posy never worked out why she desired the things, people, fashions, jobs that she did, all of them Perdita's. She never sat down and thought it through. She never consciously realised, *I want this because Perdita has it*. Her craving, her ambition overwhelmed her, blinded her to all else and she knew that person, place, thing or style was what she wanted more than anything else and she went after it with frightening determination.

Her plan that evening was quite clear and simple; she would get Larry into bed. She had divined he was an honourable man so she knew she'd have to be careful. But being honourable, she reasoned, would force him afterwards to drop Perdita in favour of her. *Then* she would be happy.

Perdita would recover. After all, they were not sleeping together. Perdita, when Posy had asked her, had blushed and shaken her head and Posy knew her friend well enough to understand that they had not as yet had sex. So, Posy reasoned, Perdita and Larry were still not, in her book, hooked up. Love was a free-for-all. Like war the victor took it all and all was fair. And Larry was, after all, a man and men were ruled by the equipment in their pants.

How she was going to get the honourable Larry into bed with her was another matter. It was a challenge. She would have to be very careful, she realised that, and shivered with sexual excitement as she asked him to carry her weekend case up to her door.

She had made sure the case was heavy. She had put a candlestick that weighed a ton in the bottom of her Samsonite carry-all. The iron candlestick was one of a pile of odds and ends Melinda had bought locally, from a house near Oak Wood Court and was going to use in a chic residence she was decorating in Maida Vale. Posy had shoved it into her soft case smiling at how heavy it made the carry-all. She looked up at Larry, helplessly appealing to his chivalry. As well as being honourable she knew that Larry would be chivalrous. Obvious. She also guessed that he responded to vulnerability and she looked up at him with practised eyes, utterly submissive and helpless.

Once in the small apartment it became easier. She told him to put the case down in the living room and went swiftly into the kitchen, leaving him standing awkwardly in the middle of the room, aware that it would be rude to just go. She poured him a brandy. She kicked off her panties and went back into the living room. She gave him the brandy and it seemed to him churlish to refuse. Inevitably, he downed it in one. He was, after all, about to leave. She, with the bottle in her hand, re-filled it instantly.

'No, no, not for me, Posy. I'm off now.' He looked around for somewhere to put the glass but there was nowhere and she did not take it from him.

'Oh, drink it up,' she said, and he quaffed it obediently.

'Hell, I'm driving,' he said and she watched him relax. He was not the type to drink very much and the quick brandies would take the edge off him, diminish those honourable instincts just a little. All this time she kept up a light chatter.

He was talking to her now about Perdita.

'It's funny how she paints her mother and father as unkind. Villains even,' he said.

'Well,' she shrugged, 'Perdita does ... exaggerate. She lives in another world, does Perdita,' she told him.

What happened next left him perplexed for the rest of his life. He was never able to explain how it happened. Afterwards he thought it would—could—be classed as rape. If the situation was reversed and he was the woman it certainly would.

She crossed the room swiftly and sat astride him. The action took him aback but his limbs responded almost automatically to her sudden proximity. She pushed him against the back of the armchair and kissed him; her body gyrating against his.

It was lust. The brandy had weakened Larry's resistance and his manhood reacted eagerly to the onslaught so that he found himself deprived of the ability to resist. She had her hands all over him. She was undoing his pants, she was exciting him, arousing him, and he was aware only of the sensations in his groin.

She was thorough. Her busy hands, her soft lips, her body against his, weakened him and he was putty in her hands. His mind was numb, all his feelings were centered elsewhere.

She got him free and pushed him into her expertly, with such force that he gasped. He felt the excitement down his legs and an unbearable erotic energy washing over him.

She impaled him and worked her body against his, moving faster and faster against him as the rising crescendo thundered in his ears then exploded as he came fiercely into her.

It all took five minutes. He sat there in the armchair dazed, unable to grasp exactly what had happened, still shaken by the force and intensity of the encounter. He had never experienced anything like it before in his life and could not grasp now how it had happened, or if it had really happened at all. Perhaps it had been an hallucination, a figment of his imagination, bizarre and frightening.

Posy left him there, picking up his glass, returning to the kitchen. She smiled to herself, a secret, satisfied smile. It was all right now. She wanted nothing more just yet. She had accomplished her purpose. All was well.

It had been easier than she had anticipated, much easier. After a moment or two, time for Larry to have recovered his equilibrium, she returned to the living room. She felt confident, in charge of the situation. She walked up to him. He was standing in front of the mantelpiece, a puzzled, worried look on his face. She kissed his lips softly. He recoiled.

'Was that good for you?' she asked, deliberately arch.

'What?' He was still frowning, perplexed.

'It was wonderful for me,' she said. 'Oh, thank you, Larry.'

'I must go . . . I must . . .'

'You'll call me, Larry, won't you?' She touched his cheek.

'Em . . .'

'I'm not the type of girl you can have a quickie with, you know. But you are not the wham-bam-thank-you-mam type, are you, who'll have his wicked way and then just leave.'

'It was more like you having your way . . . I'm sorry . . .' He could not wait to get out.

'It's no use you saying you're sorry.' Her voice was becoming harsh.

'I didn't ask you to . . . well . . . you know. What we did . . .' he stammered.

'What do you mean?' she cried, 'what are you suggesting? That I *forced* you? That I *made* you do it against your will?'

He wanted to say yes, but in his heart he knew it would not be completely true. He had, after the surprise, those initial reluctant moments, not pulled away. He should have, he knew that, but he didn't. If he had not exactly enjoyed the experience it had certainly excited him unbearably, so much so that he had not wanted her to stop.

He wanted more than anything now to leave, to get out of here. He was thoroughly upset and angry. His head was in a whirl as he ran the film of what they had done over in his mind. He thought he could chart their every move, their every word, how it had happened, but with everything she said he became more and more unsure. She was twisting things. Had he behaved inappropriately without even realising it? Had he sent signals, unaware he was doing so?

Larry, a calm, cerebral man, had never before experienced anything like this. He had had his share of amorous encounters and had felt guilt in some cases, and in some not. He'd made love to his high-school sweetheart and parted from her regretfully when she fell in love with another. But it had been straightforward and uncomplicated. He had never before been in a situation like this and he was desperate to escape it.

He stared at Posy for a moment and in that moment she was suddenly afraid. His face was pale, his lips tight, his eyes hard.

'I'm in love with Perdita,' he said.

'After that show of passion, I doubt it,' she contradicted him sweetly.

'I wouldn't call it passion,' he said, 'I'd call it lust.'

'I didn't do it on my own,' she said.

He cleared his throat. 'I've got to go,' he announced firmly. 'This thing has become . . .'

'Don't worry, Larry. I won't breathe a word to Perdy.'

'Don't call her that!' It was out before he could stop himself.

'I've always called her that! I've known her longer than you have.'

She was looking at him intently. Her eyes were very clear and he had a sudden realisation that she was far cleverer than he had given her credit for.

Perdita had warned him about her family, and about Posy and perhaps he should have listened. He had not taken her seriously enough, believing, especially after he had met them, that she was ultra-sensitive and they were not really such monsters after all. Now he was not so sure. She had told him how they made her feel and he had seen for himself her insecurity, her lack of confidence. He had chosen not to accept the fact that she had not been born that way, that someone had taken those qualities from her, had torn her down. He had allowed himself to be seduced by her father's brilliance, her mother's charm and her friend's duplicity. He cursed himself for a fool. It was all superficial, their brilliance, their charm, their deviousness, all insubstantial.

Afterwards, full of self-disgust, the actual happenings of that night changed subtly in his mind. He blamed himself. He decided he had had a mental aberration, was horrified at his venality, his weakness, his appalling lack of moral fibre. What a shit he had been. But, he felt he had learned his lesson. It would never happen again.

He flew to Egypt next morning, faxing Perdita at The Design Factory. He told her he had been called away suddenly. *I have been asked to go to Aswan urgently*, he said in the fax. *See you when I get back.*

Melinda pulled the paper out of the machine, reading it aloud. 'Oh dear, I hope we didn't frighten him off,' she remarked and Posy smiled.

CHAPTER FOURTEEN

Perdita decided to fly to Aswan and join Larry. His fax had made up her mind and suddenly it all seemed very clear to her.

She loved him and he loved her. Why then should she hang back?

She packed a case and without telling anyone hopped on a BA plane from Heathrow the morning after Larry left, two days after his visit to Oak Wood Court. She left a message on her answerphone to the effect that she had gone away and for the caller to leave a message. She faxed the Old Cataract Hotel where Larry had told her he always stayed and went to Heathrow at the crack of dawn. She closed her eyes, crossed her fingers and gave herself over to the heady sensation of leaving England for unknown and foreign shores.

Egypt, Land of the Pharaohs. She was dazzled when she landed for the sun was fiercer than she had ever known it. She found herself surrounded by robed Arabs in an unfamiliar atmosphere and the heat fell on her like a blanket.

She had thought she would be intimidated, but like the redoubtable Victorian Englishwomen who had preceeded her here to the shores of the Nile she felt only a surge of excited confidence. I'm free, she thought, I'm a free agent. There is nothing to be afraid of.

She took a taxi to the hotel and gave herself over to the totally alien atmosphere of the place. Camels, only seen before in her ancient Bible in school. Children, barefoot, begging. The Eastern buildings and the men arguing, chatting, telling their beads, sitting in the shade outside their shops. The dusty palms and above all the bustle around the huge ships on the waters of the Nile.

Entering the hotel she felt she was entering another era. The large Victorian rooms, the ceiling fans, the calm servants, the atmosphere of age-old tranquility soothed her and she went to the desk, relinquishing her case and her carryall to willing hands.

'Has Mr Burton checked in?' she asked the smiling face behind the desk at reception.

'Yes, but he is not in at the moment.'

'There is no hurry,' she told him, her voice echoing in the vast marble hall.

Her room was delightful and before she unpacked her few things, her chinos and shirts and toiletries, her black Jean Muir dress, she ordered a pot of coffee and sat at her window looking out over the Nile, sipping contentedly.

It was an amazing sight. The fellucas, their sails gleaming against the sun, the big pleasure ships that sailed the river taking passengers up and down the fertile banks. From Cairo to Luxor, Edfu and Kom Ombo to Aswan and on to Abu Simbel.

The crowds below her moved slowly but were the noisiest she had ever seen. They shouted, gesticulated, hurried on their bicycles, pulling the carts, the motley crowd ebbed and flowed like a tide past the hotel.

Why hadn't she travelled before? Why had she shut herself up, boxed herself in, close-minded, restricted, caged in her own little world, dominated by others?

She had never before felt this sense of freedom, this wild excitement in her breast. Here she was, a stranger in a strange land, utterly content and alone. She lifted her arms over her head and stretched and yawned happily and felt herself relax. 'I didn't know,' she murmured. 'I did not know that this was possible.'

Larry burst into her room a little later and swept her into his arms and kissed her and held her for dear life.

'Oh my darling, my love. Oh you don't know how good it is to see you.'

'Hey, hey,' She laughed with delight at his warm welcome. 'Easy. I'm here. I'm not going to run away.'

'Oh, my precious one,' He buried his face in her hair, then kissed her passionately and she responded as never before, all restraint gone, eager for him.

Larry's love-making was urgent and intense. Guilty and disgusted with his last performance, he wanted only to wipe away the memory of Posy and that weird erotic interlude. He loved Perdita and his love was pure and passionate and he gave her his heart as well as his body as he caressed her and urged her to release.

Perdita kept her eyes open so as not to miss one second of these wondrous moments. The man she loved, inside her, every limb entwined, utterly his. She could see the stars through the window as she came. As the sensations climaxed and her whole body shook she had her eyes wide open and she stared at the stars. There seemed to be thousands, millions very near, bright gold pinpricks blazing in the ice-cold desert night.

She thought, if I died now I would have reached Nirvana. So this is the fulfillment of love. This is what the poets rhapsodise about. This is why people die, this is why lovers are speechless or utter the old, old phrases again and again.

This is what my mother waits for from my father, waiting so hopelessly, in vain. This is why my father lives a lie and this is why Fern Morrison has been prepared to live a life of concealment, gambling with the well-being of her children.

And Perdita understood. Yes, she thought, this is worth searching the world for, dying for. This is love.

CHAPTER FIFTEEN

'I want to know about all the women in your life before me.'

'No you don't!' He thought fleetingly of Posy then dismissed that tiny cloud. It seemed a dream to him now, another world.

'Did you love any of them like you love me?'

'No. I didn't. And stop this inquisition, Perdita. It is pure insecurity and I don't want you to be insecure ever again.'

She sighed happily. 'I won't be,' she whispered, 'not after this time with you.'

They stayed in their room for two days, sending down for food. The minion who delivered their various meals smiled knowingly at them, but benignly, like an indulgent parent.

Life became unreal for Perdita. She felt herself isolated with Larry in a strange and beautiful place of the senses, a wondrous place of foreign scents and exotic foods and sounds, a place where her inner self was revealed to her, showing her to be a woman passionate and generously loving, able to give and receive. The discovery was astonishing and her ardent soul glowed as she blossomed with the fabulous acceptance of her newly found beauty. I am desired and desirable, her heart sang. I am cherished and lovely. It was amazing, and after years of believing herself unworthy to be loved the gift he gave her of her own unique beauty was a pearl beyond price.

When they eventually left the hotel they strolled along the banks of the Nile, pestered by vendors trying to push at them beads, bangles, chains, miniature sphinx, stone pyramids, King Tut masks in glorious blue and gold, but Larry and Perdita were oblivious to their pestering. Hand in hand, as lovers always are, they had eyes only for each other.

He introduced her to Yasser and they got on immediately. The Egyptian liked her total lack of artifice, her naturalness and her real interest in their work. She was outraged as he explained their work to her and became instantly converted to the cause. Larry's passion would be her passion too. But she had a natural affinity with wounded, helpless beings and her warm heart was instantly anxious to help.

'Something will have to be done, Larry,' Yasser said as they dined in the hotel one night, 'we are running out of money. We've got a huge overdraft and I'm afraid we'll have to close the refuge here in Aswan if we don't get an immediate infusion of cash.'

'Hold on, Yasser. We'll get it somehow.'

'Little dribs and drabs are no use, Larry. We need real money.'

'Tell me about it,' Perdita asked, 'explain.'

Yasser waxed eloquent over dinner and Perdita pledged her help and support. It seemed to her a wonderful opportunity to share Larry's life and interests, and something she herself was terribly interested in.

'Do you think we could get your father interested?' Larry asked casually and she did not even flinch. She realised suddenly that she no longer feared her father. Her awe of him, her sense of inferiority was gone, just like that.

'Why not?' she asked lightly. 'But it would have to come from you, Larry. He won't listen to me.'

'Can you set it up?' he inquired.

'Sure. I'll try. Nothing to lose.'

They watched the molten sun go down over the hills, the fellucas outlined darkly against the sky. They went into the desert and he took her to visit the wonderful temples, at Philae and up the river to Abu Simbel. The magnificence took her breath away. It was awe

142

inspiring and she could only marvel at her ignorance. The world was so full of wonders, stupendous man-made creations that defied time, yet revealed man's mortality as nothing else could. Humans aspiring to be God, trying to out-do the Creator.

But in the end God always won. No temple was grander than the desert itself, no ancient monument could outshine the Nile. No wonder could compare with a rose, a palm tree, no artist could match a sunset.

She said as much to Larry, who agreed with her.

'It's what your father was saying,' he said.

'Oh, him again!'

'It *was* what he said.'

'I know. Sorry, Larry. It's just that he is different with me. I don't expect you to understand.'

He thought of Posy and shuddered. 'But I do,' he contradicted her, 'I really do. However, in the context of the hospital he might be very useful to us. Let us play him at his own game, Perdita. He might find it very convenient for his image to be seen to help us. Animal welfare is a popular cause in England. Look at David Attenborough. Rolf Harris. Put it this way, Perdita, it won't hurt his image one little bit.'

'And that is very important to my father.'

'I know.'

They stayed on. Larry explained that they had a locum when either of them were away

143

from the practice.

'I get more and more absorbed here, Perdita,' he said, and she got the feeling that this was where his spiritual home was.

Perdita phoned her mother. 'Where are you, Perdita, in God's name? Why haven't you been at work? I'm sorry, but at this rate I'll have to fire you. Posy has been pleading with me not to do anything drastic . . .'

Not are you all right? Are you ill?

'I'm in Aswan, Mother.' Her voice was cool.

'Wha . . .?' Astonishment. Melinda deprived of words.

'Egypt, Mother.'

Silence. She could almost see her mother's bewilderment and she giggled, then said, 'It's okay for you to fire me. I'm not coming back to The Design Factory.'

'What?' She could hear the utter disbelief in her mother's voice. 'Are you . . .? What is happening?' Incredulity.

'I'm here with Larry, Mother. I don't want to work for you any more.' She kept her voice light. 'I've got other things to do now.' She replaced the receiver.

She had decided to work for Larry in whatever capacity he needed her and he was enthusiastic. They talked it over.

'At the moment, from what I can see, it's hit or miss,' she said, heart beating fast, 'it's amateur. Now I know amateur means you do it for love, but you need organising. I could do

144

that, I know I could.'

'You're absolutely right,' he agreed. 'We've registered, done stuff like that but both David and myself, *and* Yasser are more interested in the veterinary work than in the fund raising at which we're all hopeless.' He told her she would be very good at PR, and his belief in her did wonders for her morale.

'You would be terrific at it, Perdita. You have a natural shy, persuasive manner that disarms and I think you would be an asset. It is what we have lacked and I have been looking for.' He frowned and she stared at his face, taking in every line and curve in a loving gaze. *I adore you*, she thought, *I worship the ground you walk on.* His hairline was beaded with sweat and she wanted desperately to lick every drop away, but she sat opposite him in the large Victorian lounge sipping her tea decorously and no one would have guessed her lascivious thoughts. She was utterly content, like those bees drunk on nectar she used to see lurching about the rosebushes in Oak Wood Court, she felt dizzy with love. Her body was so relaxed it felt liquid, and she marvelled at how she'd grown.

She telephoned her father at the studio at a time when she knew he'd be available. She had never before in her life phoned him. She was quite calm as she talked to him, outlining the programme, the Cooke Hospital work, its aims, its usefulness and, above all, its appeal.

145

'You'll tug at the hearts of the British,' she said, 'you know how they love animals and how they respond to people actively involved in helping them.'

'Why do you need me?' he asked calmly. Listening to her, he was all business.

'We need funds. You are high profile. Your name would be invaluable to us. Could you give us a mention in the *Hastings Hour*? It's a bit hopeless when we have to rely on garden parties arranged by Larry's mum and local events haphazardly put on to raise funds.'

'Mmmm.'

'At the moment only people in the know, and that's not too many, are organising events to raise money. Your name would uplift the whole undertaking to national status.'

'Really, Perdita, I never knew you had such a high opinion of me.'

She did not get hurt or angry, did not stammer or stutter, simply said calmly. 'I don't. We're not talking about my opinion of you. I'm simply stating the fact that you are a public figure with immense pull. So was Hitler!' She heard him laugh loudly. 'Will you help?' she asked.

'Yes,' he said incisively, much to her surprise. 'You let me know what you have. Send me the bumph. A video would be helpful. Get Larry to do interviews. I remember thinking he would be camera-friendly. He's got a good, strong face. Have him talk to us about it. You know, shirt unbuttoned, sleeves rolled up, hair tousled, that sort of thing. Heart-wrenching, animals in pitiful states. I'll give you a five, ten minute profile on the programme.'

'When?'

'About June? Okay?'

'Sure.'

'And be here to take the feedback. When I do something there's a hell of a lot of feedback and I'm bloody well not dealing with it. ''Bye.'

They whooped. They danced around the hotel room like dervishes. He lifted her up, twirled her, whirled her about in his arms and they made love.

They spent the next month filming the Cooke Hospital: its work, the people, the animals there. What Perdita saw impressed her and the video was remarkable.

'It's very good, Larry. Not at all sentimental. It should shock and move people but it is not sensationalist or gratuitous. And you've done what my father wanted. You look great presenting it.'

'You'd think that anyhow because you're mad about me.' He turned, laughing, but pleased too, she could see.

'Is David okay about us being here so long?' she asked.

'Sure.' He smiled. 'He's a bit jealous. Thinks you've taken his place a bit.'

'Oh gosh, Larry I . . .'

'It was bound to happen. But he'll get over it.

I've suggested he do a video and you try to get Rolf Harris or David Attenborough to front it.'

Perdita frowned. 'I'm afraid not, Larry. This has nothing to do with the fact that I love you, but you are perfect fronting the video we've done and I want people to associate you with the project. We don't want them muddled. As my father said, you are camera-friendly. You come over great. You'll have them opening their wallets. Putting David Attenborough or other big names in now would only confuse the issue.'

'David's not going to be over the moon about all this, but I reasoned with him and I'm afraid he'll just have to accept what's best for the hospital.' He stared into space, a worried frown on his face, then glanced back at her, smiling suddenly. 'Well, it can't be helped. I'll sort him out when we get back.'

She did not want to leave Egypt. Never in her life had she been as happy as she was in Aswan.

They dined with Yasser that last night in the Old Cataract Hotel, in the fading grandeur of the lofty, chandelier-lit dining room. They were a joyful party, celebrating the end of their most pressing problem, the beginning of new hope. They toasted each other and their commitment to the Cooke's Hospital with new optimism and when Larry and Perdita went to bed that night they were a little tipsy, and oh so happy.

'Will all this change in London?' she asked a

little tremulously.

He took her face between his hands and smiled at her anxiety. 'Of course not, my darling,' he assured her, 'I love you, I always will. And we have a lot to do, you and I.'

But it did change. It changed drastically in a way neither of them could have foreseen.

CHAPTER SIXTEEN

The programme went out and the response was overwhelming, exceeding their wildest dreams.

Perdita had returned to the flat. She had expected Larry to move in with her, or that she would move in with him, but he explained that she would be uncomfortable in his one-room pad over the surgery and suggested they look for a place together.

'But let's wait until after the programme goes out, my love, we've got too much on our plates before then. Besides, I have to involve David, spend a little time with him. Placate him. After all, we've left him out completely. He has no function in the project so he'll be miffed and I don't blame him.'

'If it had been the other way around I cannot see you being upset. I think you'd only be interested in what was best for the hospitals.'

'Well, he's younger than I am.' Larry shrugged. 'Maybe I'm overdoing it. I would have been glad he was getting the hospital help. Yes.'

The project, once rolling, took all their time. There was so much to be done, more than either of them realised. Lucas was gleeful. 'Now you know how hard I work,' he crowed to a harassed Perdita, 'people think my job is simply standing in front of the camera. Well, now you know it's not!'

Larry had to film an interview with Lucas and Perdita, who provided the data and the history of Cooke's Hospital for Animals, had not only to familiarise herself with everything about the project, but she spent a great deal of time faxing, phoning and writing this information for the studio.

'How many times do I have to tell them?' she asked Larry on one of the few occasions they were able to get together, albeit in a crowded studio with a full crew looking on.

'As many times as it takes,' he told her, smiling at her, adding in a whisper, 'I miss you so. How I miss you!'

'Do they lose my faxes or something?' she asked, murmuring back, 'Me too. Oh, Larry, you're starving me, why?'

'I dunno whether they lose them or not, but it's worth it. Oh, it's worth it.' He took her hands in his. 'We'll be together soon, my dearest. At the moment this is my priority. I don't know whether you realise how grateful I am,' he told her earnestly, 'This is my life's work. My dream. My *raison d'être*.'

'But it isn't only gratitude, that you feel for me, is it?' she inquired anxiously.

'Oh, my darling, how can you think that?'

'I don't. Not really.'

'You've got to learn to trust me.'

'I do. I do.'

And then there was silence and a great void.

Perdita was busy night and day with the overwhelming response to the programme. Letters, faxes, receipts to be sent, phonecalls, correspondence to people as far as Penzance and Edinburgh, from all over the British Isles stuff kept pouring in. Lucas was right, the feedback was astonishing. She had queries to reply to, informative leaflets to send out and sometimes she had to research questions and find accurate answers. The e-mail, the faxes, the phone calls, the questions, the donations, all had to be dealt with and Perdita was too new at the business, too anxious to get it right to delegate, and Larry was nowhere in sight.

At first it did not worry her. There was so much going on. Worn to a frazzle, yet exhilarated and excited, she phoned him once or twice after she got home but there was no reply, only his answerphone taking messages.

She could not seem to reach him on his bleeper either, nor his mobile and God knows she tried. Still not alarmed she sent faxes to the surgery informing him of the fabulous amounts donated, sure he was thrilled by the public's

151

generosity, needing his congratulations. Each night she fell into a dreamless sleep, too tired to miss him too much, trusting him as he had asked her to.

It was the beginning of the second week after the programme and things were starting to slow down a little when she began to worry and it suddenly seemed distinctly odd that there had been no word from him, no response to her messages. No communication at all.

Then David came to see her and dropped the bombshell.

She had thought it was Larry when the knock came to her door. She rushed to open it, her heart skipping at the thought of seeing him, hearing his voice, feeling his arms around her. So she was surprised to see David there, but not alarmed. He was probably going to have a little moan to her and maybe ask her to give him a look-in to the Cooke Hospital thing. After all it was his project as much as Larry's. He was entitled.

He stood in her little living room looking awkward and ill at ease. She decided she was right and he was going to talk about the project and how he'd been overlooked when he said, 'There's no easy way to say this Perdita . . .' he paused. She knew then that Larry was dead. He'd had an accident. He was hurt, needed her.

'It's Larry,' she cried, everything in her shaking in anguish, 'he's . . . he's . . .'

'Oh God, my dear, he's going to marry Posy.'

She giggled, relief flooding her. 'Don't be daft, David. They hardly know each other.' Then she saw his face and felt her heart stop a second. She sat down abruptly. 'That was sick!' she whispered through lips that were suddenly dry. 'You sick bastard. How could you joke like that? Play such a trick on me? What a foul thing to say.'

'It's true, Perdita. I wish it wasn't. I promise you I'd never do that to you. Unfortunately it is true.'

'It's a lie! It's a lie!' she shouted.

'Why would I lie to you?'

'Because you're jealous of Larry. The publicity he's getting. You're jealous because I love him. You want to spoil . . .' Even as she spoke she knew what she was saying wasn't true.

'No, my dear. You know that's not true. You know this thing is not a competition. It's about helping the animals. I don't really care how or who gets it done as long as it *is* done. Anyhow, you know I wouldn't do something like that.'

Then she said helplessly, 'Why? How?' accepting it, wanting to understand.

'I don't know. He won't say. He can't. He doesn't want to see you. He says he couldn't bear it.'

She shook her head, her world crumbling around her, falling down, crashing down, breaking up into little pieces. 'No, no. It's not true! It can't be!'

All those nights in Egypt, in that bed, wrapped in his arms. All that love, that passion. She had heard that when drowning your past flashes through your mind and now all she could see were pictures of the past running through her head like a television screen. Her father's face: 'You look awful in that colour Perdita, but then not many colours suit you.' Her mother: 'You must get something done with your hair, Perdita, it's so straggly.' Her father: 'Your skin is not your best asset, Perdita.' Her mother again: 'You're so clumsy, Perdita, do you have to drop *everything*?' Her father; 'I don't know where we got you, Perdita, I really don't. You have nothing in common with either of us.'

And then Larry: 'You're perfect!' 'I love you.' 'You are beautiful!' 'Never say that again! I won't have you put yourself down.'

She shivered. David had made a mistake, a terrible mistake. 'Where is he? I want to see him.' She stood up and started for the door.

'He does not want to see you.' David stopped her. 'Here.'

'What's this?'

'He said to give you this.'

It was a sheet of notepaper. No envelope. It was his handwriting and the distinctive signature. It said:

'I can never see you again as my love. I cannot explain, don't ask me to. I have no choice, my dear. Just forget about me. I don't deserve you. Please do not get in touch, it would not change things and would only cause you pain.

Larry Burton.'

She read it three times, maybe four. The blood rushed to her head, then ebbed away and she fainted, slipping unconscious to the ground before David could catch her.

CHAPTER SEVENTEEN

David stayed with her for the next week. He was always there. He gave her a sedative at night and slept on the sofa in the living room.

Afterwards he told her he was afraid she would try to kill herself and she replied she had wanted to, wanted to badly, desperately wanted to leave this planet, turn out the light on her life, feel nothing more. Time was a blur, a nightmare. Engulfed by an unbearable loneliness and pain, a feeling of complete betrayal, the days passed infinitely slowly. Deep, deep, heavy-footed moment by lingering moment, time ticked slowly by, an eternity of long drawn out, agonising seconds passing leadenly.

Her mother phoned. Listlessly she took the mobile from David. 'I hear your chap has got engaged to Posy,' her mother's voice held a note of vindication as if, Perdita thought she had warned her daughter of some perfidity, some calamity.

'Yes,' Perdita said.

'Oh, Perdita, when will you learn . . .' Perdita switched the phone off abruptly. She did the same thing on Posy.

She could not believe that Posy would ring her, but her friend did, bubbling over, excited.

'I'm so happy, Perdita. I'm only sorry about you, if you are upset . . .' *Upset!* Her heart was breaking! *Upset!* 'I know you two were seeing each other . . .' *Seeing each other!* Bodies entwined in the silver light of an Egyptian night, the golden warmth of an Egyptian day. Kisses sweeter than wine. Nights and days of passion. *Seeing each other!* Perdita shook with angry tension. '. . . but Larry tells me it is over so I moved in. I can't say I'm proud, Perdy, of what I've done, but I love him.' You *want* him, you mean, Perdita thought. 'I don't want to lose your friendship, Perdy, I really don't . . .'

Perdita cut her off. *Click.* Like that. End of friendship. If it had ever been one. She wondered about that now. She hated Posy, hated what she had done, wanting her to be dead.

Had Posy ever been her friend? Perdita, in those dark nights and days deplored her own weakness, her naïvety. She had, she realised given permission to others to abuse her, use

156

her, prey on her. But she had been brought up like that. It had been the crucible of her existence. She had known no better.

'I've no backbone, David,' she sobbed one night when tears eventually came, like a benediction, dissolving the knot in her chest. 'I'm so weak. I *hate* saying no to anyone, particularly those close to me.'

She wept, cried, wailed and wallowed for twenty-four hours, sobbing away her hatred, her fury, her resentment, leaving only an enormous regret.

'I know,' David had answered her.

'No you don't!' she cried angrily. 'You haven't a clue what it's like to love and have that love rejected. I lived in hope, all my life, hoping I'd get the love I so much needed from my parents and I waited in vain. I *longed* for them to love me. Ached. They never did. Fern adores you, anyone can see that. And what's more she *approves* of you.'

'Yes she does. And it is hard that yours didn't, Perdita. But you'll have to get over it. Move on. Not let them defeat you.'

'*They* didn't defeat me, David. Larry did,' she told him helplessly.

'Have some brandy, it will relax you.'

'Don't like brandy,' she replied stubbornly.

'Nevertheless, have some.'

She looked up at him with tear-washed eyes. 'You've been so good to me, David, over these weeks,' she told him.

157

'Oh I've got an ulterior motive,' he said jokingly, but seriously too, making her nervous.

'Like a brother,' she said, then asked because she wanted to know, 'Who is doing your work, David? You've been with me here most of the time these last weeks. Is Larry in the surgery?'

David turned his back and poured the drink. 'Yes, he is. Well, he had that long break in Egypt, didn't he? So now he's at the practice with the locum and I'm here.'

Perdita smiled sadly. 'That long break! Was that what it was to him? A break in Egypt?' The pain returned like knives in her breast. 'Oh, David, where did I go wrong?'

He shook his head helplessly. They had been over and over this so many times. 'I don't *know*,' he said and gave her the brandy.

'Is she so much more desirable than I am?'

He knew whom she meant. 'No. She's a bitch. It's partly your own fault Perdita, for letting her into your life.'

'I couldn't say no.' She smiled sadly, then gulped the brandy down. 'I see now that she wanted what I had. Though why anyone would want that I cannot understand.'

'She only saw the appearence of what you had, not the actuality,' he said.

'She took from me all those years, took from my mother and my father and from me.'

'She took your confidence, Perdita. She tried to steal your soul.'

158

'Well, she's succeeded. She's broken my heart, my soul, my spirit. I have nothing left.'

'No, Perdita, as you said, Larry did that.'

She let out a long, jagged breath and nodded. 'Yes. I suppose so,' she said.

'You mustn't let them destroy you, Perdita. What you have to do now is to put it all behind you. It's difficult I know but you must.'

She stared at him, eyes wide. 'You think it's that easy?' she cried.

'No,' he sighed, 'no I don't, but you have to *try*. For the first time in your life, Perdita, you have to stop bowing down in defeat. It's habit, Perdita, *habit*. You must try, a day at a time to evict Larry and Posy out of your head.' He pulled her around to face him. 'Listen, Perdita, you think it's the end of the world now, well, it is not! Larry and Posy are filling your mind. They are living there at the moment. You have given them space. House-room. Now is the time to put them out. It will take time, hard work. I never said it would be easy, but it gives you something to do. A task.'

'How do you know so much about it?' she asked.

He smiled. 'Oh, I've had experience,' he said. 'Every time they come into your head . . .'

'Which is all the time,'

'Change the disc. Push them out. Otherwise they'll haunt you. Come between you and your work, your sleep, your every waking thought. You have to be ruthless with yourself and start at once.'

She nodded. It made sense but only because Posy was in there with Larry, in her head. She'd never have wanted to evict Larry. Posy was, however, another matter and she knew those thoughts of Posy and Larry would drive her mad. Posy doing things with him that she had done. Posy in his arms. No, that was torture. Pure hell. She would do anything to pluck that out, give herself respite from that particular agony.

'What am I going to do, David?' she asked him piteously, 'what's going to happen to me? I don't think I can bear it.'

'You're going to survive, Perdita. Start by taking my advice. Get them out and free yourself. This won't last forever, believe it or not.'

'A bit of me wants to,' she looked at him appealingly, 'A bit of me nurtures the pain. It means he's still *there*. Part of me. When it goes it really will be over. I'll be desolate then. Empty. Maybe forever.'

'No. You'll be ready for a refill. Ready for a new love. And I'll be there. Waiting. Oh Perdita, you know how I feel . . .'

She shook her head vehemently. 'No! No, David, you must never . . . you must not think . . .'

'I'm sorry. Oh God, Perdita, how awfully crass of me. So soon. Oh forgive me. But I will wait. I mean it. I'll wait for you.'

'No, listen, David, you must listen. It's not possible. It's *never* going to be possible.' She was adamant. He looked at her, frowning. 'But why? Why not, for Pete's sake?'

'I can't tell you. I can't.'

He left it at that for the moment deciding it was much too soon after her break with Larry, that he was rushing things, being insensitive.

He took her out regularly to dinner and entertained her with his stories of the practice. She winced every time he mentioned Larry but it was inevitable that he should figure largely in David's tales of animal adventures and amusing anecdotes. After all, he was the partner and David did not want to avoid any mention of him completely because he hoped she'd gradually accept the idea of Larry and Posy and the wound would heal leaving the path open and clear for him.

After all, he'd seen her first. She had been his choice. Then Larry with his brilliant smile, his charm, his shy manner, that manner that seduced all their female clients and made him, inevitably, their first choice, had stepped in and led her astray for a short, oh so short a time. Couple of months. What was that in the long years of a life? Nothing.

She had begun to rely on him, he could see that. Sometimes he coaxed a smile from her and sometimes as the weeks passed, a laugh.

He told her they wanted her to continue her PR work for Cooke's Hospital. At first, in her shock and despair, she rejected the idea out of hand, but David talked her round. 'You have to learn to face the situation, Perdita. Larry is still on this planet. Pretending he doesn't exist will not do you any good. In order to recover you have to come to terms with it.' He smiled at her over the rim of his glass, 'And it is a job you are very good at.'

She nodded. 'I loved it,' she agreed.

'You did fantastic work for us. The cheques are still coming in.'

'That was my father,' she said.

'There you go again!' He shook his head, exasperated. 'Running your contribution down. Another habit you'll have to break.' He leaned forward over the table. 'Look, Perdita, this job really excites you. I can see that. It would be cutting off your nose to spite your face to quit now. You can keep out of Larry's way. He'll be anxious not to confront you anyhow. He'll not be too happy to have you in his face and so much of your work can be done alone.' He grinned at her though her heart was crying at his words. 'Or with me,' he said.

She knew it was dangerous. Both men were dangerous to her, but she loved the job. It made her feel successful, something she had never felt before, and she felt at last she was doing something worthwhile. The Cooke Hospital really mattered to her. It inspired her.

But it was not only that. Her motives were not strictly pure. She wanted to have *something* to do with Larry, his job if not his bed. She needed, in spite of what David said, some connection, a tie she did not want to sever.

There was a mountain of work awaiting her. She clocked in at the BBC to clear up the last of the correspondence and met her father quite by accident. He seemed surprised to see her.

'Posy's been looking for you,' he said without preamble.

'Oh!' she kept her voice calm and the fact that she achieved even this gave her confidence. 'What on earth for?'

'To be her bridesmaid. She wants you to be bridesmaid at her wedding.' There was a malicious gleam in his eyes that angered Perdita and she managed to reply lightly, 'Sure! Tell her I'd be glad. Delighted.' She was rewarded by his surprise. 'But I'm busy, Father, can't talk now. Got to go.'

'I didn't think you'd want to go on working on the project,' he persisted, 'after Larry dumped you.'

Again, that terrible pain, fierce and stabbing in her chest. 'Why on earth not?' she asked airily, wide-eyed, puzzled. I'm doing okay, she thought. David was right. He'd told her to act until it became real. 'I like this job much better than the one I had in The Design Factory with Mother ordering me about all the time. And I'm bloody good at it,' she retorted. She could see the astonishment on his face again as she breezed away from him, crying, 'Hi Benny,' to

163

the man on the desk and waving her hand. 'Hi Babs,' she called to the girl at reception.

She allowed the job to take her over and working hard occupied all her time and what little emotion she had left was spent on the distressed animals in the Cooke Hospital. A lot of her grieving was channelled into their plight. She also took a crash course in the RSPCA First Aid for animals and general knowledge about how to care for and treat them.

She threw herself into the project, organising parties, flag days, sorting out a calendar timetable, promoting publicity and fund-raising events. She was careful with the money they'd received, sending Yasser a hefty cheque to support the Aswan hospital and organising a video of him, taking the viewer around the hospital, showing how the money was being spent, the work to be done and what was needed.

Perdita rail-roaded her father into doing a follow-up on *Hastings' Hour*, thanking the viewers, showing the video of Yasser and giving a detailed report of where their money went and how it had helped. They showed the viewers the hospitals in Cairo and Luxor as well as the one that had been threatened in Aswan.

'It's the donkeys that do it every time,' Lucas said. 'Poor, overworked, starving creatures. They look cute and pathetic at the same time. Show them a poor starving snake or ant-eater and they wouldn't give you a penny!'

'I don't know whether this job's made you callous beyond belief, Father, or were you always like that?' Perdita asked coldly.

'Don't tell me you really give a shit about those creatures, Perdita,' he said, one eye on her.

'As a matter of fact, Father, I do.'

'Oh! And I thought it was a ploy to get back at your mother and me.' He laughed. 'And maybe retrieve Larry from Posy.'

'No, Father. None of you are that important in my life any more,' she retorted.

'Wow! The kitten has grown into a cat that can scratch,' he said laughing. She met his eyes and saw a spark of admiration there. 'And what about Larry? Maybe you don't want to sever the tie,' he remarked shrewdly.

But she tossed her head, 'Larry chose Posy. His bad luck!' she cried and Lucas threw back his head and guffawed.

She didn't see Larry. He kept well away. Now and again she got a fax relating to the project from him, but nothing personal.

Bit by bit the initial pain receded. Little by little the shock of rejection, of love spurned waned. Life, her job, being so busy helped to heal her. But though the immediacy of the hurt was soothed, underneath it all Larry stayed firmly fixed deep in her heart, lodged there, beloved and cherished, hurting her constantly and the awful ache of her love for him never really disappeared.

She presented a cheerful face to the world. She took David's advice and practised replacing her anger and pain, her sadness and frustration with work. She was galvanised into action, sorting out the problems, solving the puzzles, and it worked. After her orgy of self-pity and grieving it all slipped away and the pain and anger diminished. Nothing lasts at an acute level for ever.

But Larry stayed. She did not seem able to dislodge him and much as she wanted to she could not hate him.

He was her love. He would always be.

CHAPTER EIGHTEEN

Perdita began to be aware that, in a way she was doing to David what Larry had done to her. She was dining with him, going to the theatre with him, for walks or just sitting in cafes drinking cappucino or idling in the cool dimness of the pubs on the river he loved, sipping lager and talking, mainly about the Cooke Hospital. She was sharing a lot of her time with him and to her horror she realised that he was becoming too close for comfort. Much too close.

She did not really think of him as a brother—well, half-brother—but when he looked at her there was passion in his eyes, and desire.

She had decided to go back to Egypt again. 'I want to lay the ghost,' she told David, 'and it's important for the work that I know exactly what's going on there. But for my own sake too. I don't want to turn what happened there into an idyll. Romance with a capital R.' She was being flippant, but she meant it nevertheless. Also, she wanted to get away from David for a while. He was getting to be a habit, becoming an essential part of her life. It would have been okay if they could have simply remained friends, but she knew David would not be content with that for long. She dreaded having to break with him and she was apprehensive about how she would cope without him. So she decided to go to Egypt.

Yasser wrote. He told her not to come to Karnak as he would be in Luxor. He said the heat was intense.

It's too hot for you, try to come in October or November. In the meantime I will, on Larry's instructions send a precise rendering of exactly where every penny has gone, how much has been sent to Alexandria, to Cairo and to Karnak and Luxor. They will send you videos of progress made. I cannot express my gratitude for all that you are doing to aid the cause. I have to say, dear Perdita, that whatever went wrong between you and Larry should be righted. You were a radiant couple, so suited, in my humble opinion, to each other and when Larry wrote me it was over between you I was very sad. I hope you find a way to, how do you say in English? Bury your differences.

The letter made her cry. The paper seemed to smell of the desert, of sand and the Nile. Those precious memories rushed back and she could see the thick and sparkling inlay of stars and feel her body respond so ardently to the man she loved.

Things came to a head in August. The summer in London may not have scorched like the Egyptian one, but it too was unbearably hot. Perdita felt prickly and irritable and at odds with herself. She felt as if she was waiting, for what she did not know, but *something* to happen. Posy had sent Perdita a wedding invitation with a note that read,

'Your father says you'll be my bridesmaid, Perdy, and I'm so happy. We do after all go back a long way. It would not be the same without my dearest and best friend. I'll send you the dress—don't worry, I know your measurements.'

David said, 'Don't go, Perdita. You don't have to do this.'

He sat in the armchair he always sat in when he came to her flat. He would arrive and plonk himself down in it automatically, reminding her of his assumption of intimacy, and her permission. But how could she discourage him yet still keep his friendship while he remained in ignorance of their true relationship?

She shook her head. 'Oh, but I must go,' she told him, 'It's like an end, David. The End. *Finito*. I *have* to see them tie the knot with my own eyes.'

'Don't be bitter, Perdita. It will corrode your soul.'

'I'm not,' she contradicted him, 'I'm being realistic. When I see them exchange their vows I'll be sure the whole thing is over for me forever.'

She was curled up on the sofa, the Cooke Hospital correspondence littered the floor and the table all around her and there was a half drunk glass of white wine beside her.

'You told me to face up to it and I have. I feel a lot better about it now, David, but I won't believe in the *reality* of it until I see with my own eyes the two of them saying "I do".'

'Then there'll be hope for me?' His voice shook a little and she bit her lip. 'No, David,' she cried, exasperated, 'I *told* you and told you. No. There can never be anything between us.'

'Why, Perdy, why?' he persisted. 'I know I'm not Larry. I don't expect that "first fine careless rapture" to repeat itself for you, but a more solid relationship built on loving kindness, surely that should be possible? Give it a try at least. Come on, Perdita,' he coaxed, 'consideration. Faithfulness. We have the same interests. We're never short of conversation. Our tastes are similar, haven't you noticed? All this time and we've never quarrelled. We are always in tune.'

'Like brother and sister,' she said softly.

'Oh no! What I feel for you is not brotherly. I adore you, Perdita and I think we'd make the perfect couple.'

'No, David. It's impossible. Put it out of your mind forever.'

He rose swiftly and in an instant was beside her kissing her, his lips tender on her cheek, then on her mouth, his ardour deepening into passion.

She pushed him away violently, shrinking back, her eyes horror-filled.

'No, David, *no!*' she gasped.

Surprised at how appalled she was he cried, 'Hey! I'm not Frankenstein's monster, for God's sake. I'm just a chap who loves you. What's *wrong*, Perdita?'

'*We are!*' It was out before she could stop herself. 'We *are* brother and sister, David. Well, half-brother and sister.' She jumped up off the sofa as he recoiled in shocked surprise at her words. 'Oh, David, I never meant to tell you. I promised your mother . . .'

'My *mother*?'

'Yes. She doesn't want your father to know. He thinks he's your father, but he isn't. Lucas

170

Hastings, my father is. You and Miranda. Now you see why . . .' She wrung her hands together in distress. 'Oh, I didn't mean to say anything about it, but—'

'Jesus, Perdita, have you gone *mad*? What the hell are you talking about?' He sounded so angry, and she was suddenly frightened. She had expected him to be upset, yes, but he was raging. His eyes were blazing, murderous. She twisted her hands together in anguish and cried out to him, 'It's true, David. Oh, I'm sorry, so sorry. Don't let your mother know I told you.'

She knew it was a stupid demand and she was babbling. How could he obey her? He was much too close to his mother for there to be deception. He was bound to confront her with this shocking revelation.

'Oh, I didn't want to tell you,' she cried contritely, 'break my word. But I *had* to, don't you see? You were going to make love to me.' Distressed she went on twisting her fingers together, wringing her hands, unable to think how to make things better.

'Jesus, I'm not surprised Larry broke off with you. I couldn't think why he behaved the way he did, but now I know. What a fertile imagination you've got. Of all the sick, *sick* jokes . . .'

'It's *not* a joke.'

'It's sick!' he hissed at her, 'sick. *You* must be sick. My God, how could you invent such an evil story? How could you even *think* such a thing. It really takes a weird person to dream up such a lot of garbage.'

He was so furious. She had never seen him as angry. He stood over her, towering, his body shaking. There was a white line around his mouth and his skin had lost its colour. His red hair flamed and his eyes were wild.

'It's the truth,' she insisted.

'No way!' he shouted and grunting in disgust he left the apartment abruptly, slamming the door behind him.

Where would he go? she wondered. Then she decided he would, of course, go to his mother. In a panic she phoned Fern but there was no reply.

Perdita sat, arms around her legs, wringing her hands endlessly, shaking her head, whispering to herself, 'What have I done, oh what have I done?' and finding no answer at all.

CHAPTER NINETEEN

David hurried home, his head in a whirl. He was certain Perdita, for whatever reason, was lying. Was she mentally disturbed? Had Larry discovered it and broken with her? Was she insane? She was obviously lying, but why? Maybe she'd invented this horrible story to get back at Larry, as some sort of elaborate excuse so that he wouldn't make love to her? Why on

172

earth would she think of such a thing? Why on earth would she mind that much, him making love to her? She would know he would not force her to do anything she didn't want to do, so why this terrible lie? It was such a far-fetched *foul* story and had to be, simply had to be, the product of a weird mind.

Had they mis-read her completely? David thought of all those stories about her mother and father being monsters. But Larry had said they were charming and her father had gone out of his way to help her with the Cooke Hospital project. Perhaps Perdita was warped, mentally twisted. Was that why Larry had run from her like a scalded cat?

And yet. And yet.

It fitted. In some strange way it was almost as if he'd been aware that for years there had been some secret, something not quite true about the happy families they played. He'd never wanted to dig, never wanted to enquire about certain things at home.

Like why he had never felt an ounce of identification with his father. He had assumed that it was because of his illness, an illness now so far advanced as to make his father uncommunicable. He knew his mother had someone else but he had been very careful not to find out who it was. It had not however occurred to him that he might not be Paul Morrison's son, that this other man in his mother's life might have fathered him. He had never considered that at all and, even if he had, he would not have wanted to know.

But Lucas Hastings! Dear God, Lucas Hastings.

He drove recklessly, double-parked outside the house. He opened the front door quietly. There was no one in the living-room. His father, bedridden now, would be in his own room.

David leapt up the stairs two at a time and, knocking gently at the door of his mother's bedroom, opened it.

There was his mother, in bed, naked in the filtered light through the slatted Venetian blinds. It striped her like a golden zebra. And in her arms lay the equally naked Lucas Hastings.

For a moment all was absolutely still, frozen. Nothing moved. Then David gasped as if his chest would burst and Fern raised her arms over her face as if to hide it. 'Oh no!' she whispered softly, 'oh, please God, no.' Lucas rolled over on his side and stared at David as if his interruption was just an inconvenience.

'Shit,' Lucas muttered. 'Oh damn!'

The anger David felt throbbed in his temples but no words came. Huge, overpowering waves of fury shook his body like a palsy and he knew that if there had been a gun nearby he would have used it. It was as if the David he knew, the pacifist David, the body he lived inside, had inhabited all these years, had vanished and he

174

had been taken over by some powerfully dark and evil presence. He knew now how people could kill.

Shaking, he closed the door. He knew that the scene would never be erased from his mind. He knew that his life had been changed forever. He knew that something, a purity, an innocence, a spontaneous gaiety and trust had been killed that day and was lost forever. From now on everything would be coloured by the events of that day. Every memory was tainted by what had happened. Everything he did or said, everything he remembered, every assumption he made, every word his mother had ever spoken to him had been based on a lie, on misinformation, on adultery and lust. How could he ever trust anyone ever again?

How long he stood outside the door, shaking, watching fond memories die one by one like the leaves in autumn, he did not know. He went to his father's room. The door was ajar and his father lay in bed propped up with pillows. There was spittle on his chin and the nurse who came to look after him wiped it carefully away. Did she know what was going on down the corridor? She was a lovely, compassionate Irish girl, thick-bodied, patient and slow-moving. Did she know all about his mother's love in the afternoon? No, he contradicted himself, no, *sex* in the afternoon. It wasn't love. He wouldn't dignify it with the name of love. It was not what he felt for . . . Oh,

Jesus! Perdita! No, no!

'He's quiet, sir.' The girl looked around and smiled at him and suddenly David wanted desperately to make love to her, to forget himself completely in an erotic encounter with her motherly breasts and swelling hips that would dull his senses, kill the pain if only for a moment, give him surcease. The girl had pale skin and freckles all across her nose and her hair was coarse and black. He wanted to touch it, kiss her wide generous mouth, to affirm something. Make a statement. Reassert himself. He wanted to lose himself in the sex act with this soft Irish girl with the sympathetic eyes as if by so doing he would wash away his father's sickness, his mother's guilt and Perdita's involvement in it all. Horrified by these thoughts he left the room.

His father was incapable of helping him. It did not occur to him that the same truth applied to his mother.

CHAPTER TWENTY

What had happened forced Perdita to push the past away. She had no choice, it was sink or swim time. She took stock.

David and Larry no longer loved her. That was certain. Posy had never really been her friend, she saw that clearly now. Her mother actually disliked her. She would not use the word hate, it was too strong, too close to love to be applied to what Melinda felt for her daughter.

That left only Lucas and she believed that her father had always resented her, blamed her for his forced separation from Fern, David and Miranda where his true love lay. If it hadn't been for her he would not be with Melinda now, he would be with them.

So, she told herself realistically, she had no one. There was no one. And it had to be her fault. She was somehow incapable of having a relationship, of being loved. She faced the fact, doing what David had told her to do. Being firm with herself and unsentimental.

She had a job. An inspiring job. A job she loved and the animals did not reject her. She had a niche, a path to follow and that was what she decided to do. Pull yourself together girl, she told herself, get on with it.

She threw herself into her work with energy, vigour and all the pent-up love she had a surplus of and no one seemed to want. Despite the heat, she went to Egypt. Despite Yassar's warnings. She went to Cairo and Alexandria, to Luxor and Edfu and, crossing the Sinai desert, to Jordan, Amman and Petra. There were branches of the Cooke Hospital for Animals everywhere.

It was a gruelling journey in the heat, on overcrowded planes and on horseback, in uncomfortable and rickety jeeps and all without Yassar's help. She sweated in the shade, drank gallons of bottled water, doggedly ploughed on and on in a kind of daze, determined to get firsthand knowledge, to understand, to give herself body and soul to this mission.

The desert was unrelentingly demanding. It sucked her dry then filled her with a sort of spiritual fulfilment that changed her. It forced her to look at herself calmly, almost clinically. Under a carpet of stars so brilliant that they lit up the landscape so that the desert looked like a shimmering day, she sat, cross-legged and did not dislike what she saw inside herself. Her faults were ones of humanity, abundance of love, ardour and passion. She was not disgusted by herself, saw no meanness there and did not, as she had done previously, turn away in disgust. Eventually, she began to like herself and admire the spirit within herself, her soul, her centre.

She was excited too, in spite of the heat, the insect bites and her gippy tummy, excited by the hospitals, the work done there.

She was greeted with delight by the veterinary surgeons who met her and who introduced her to their assistants, farriers and supporting staffs. These people made a great fuss of her, delighted by her interest and eager to educate her. They also pleaded for more money which she was able to promise them.

She got quite expert at diagnosis and travelled in the mobile clinic with them, wise enough not to interfere, ready to stand back and watch and learn from the experts.

She loved the animals—mainly horses, donkeys and mules—that they treated. But there were dogs too, and cats. Sometimes she nursed a gazelle in her arms. Hurt and frightened, in need of her compassion, separated from their mother she embraced all the poor, wounded frightened creatures they cared for.

All of the people with Cooke's had a single aim. To help and heal and try to make the plight of these maimed creatures easier, better and educate their owners.

There were examples of unbelievable cruelty that shocked her but she learned to keep the tears back and get on with the job. Do what she could and leave the rest.

She met kindness and gratitude everywhere she went. She helped out with a mare foaling and assisted at the humane putting to sleep of a donkey beaten half to death and covered in sores.

They called her Golden Isis, after the goddess of love and divine power. She grew bone-lean and tanned, her skin hardening under the relentless sun. She toughened up inside too and as the time passed and Posy's autumn wedding day neared, it became clearer and clearer to her what her aims were, where

179

her priorities lay. No longer tentative, no longer doubtful, no longer needing the approval of others, she decided she would return to England for Posy's and Larry's nuptials, then she would come back here to Egypt. Return to work, to labour in this, her chosen field because it inspired her. She was impervious to heat and dust, the flies and discomfort, and she realised slowly and with relief that whatever cards life had dealt her up to now, however unloving, harsh, cruel even, her parents had been, however badly Larry had treated her, however thoughtlessly cruel, inconsiderate, clumsy and feeble she had been with David and, lastly, however badly she had suffered at Posy's hands, all of it, all the components had brought her to this point, had been her preparation for this pathway that she wanted so badly to tread. Her life, if lived another way, might not have readied her for this most precious experience. The cruelty she had suffered had given her the compassion needed for the job, the eyes to see and the ears to hear the requirements. She had needed it all, the people close to her, their behaviour, their indifference, their carelessness of her feelings, and eventually Larry's introduction to Yasser and the Cooke Hospital for Animals. The events of her life were all needed to get her here where she wanted to be, here where she could find fulfilment and peace within herself and, most of all, a sweet content in her purpose.

She wiped her forehead with her arm, then holding the end of her white cotton shirt flapped it in and out to try to circulate some air around her burning body. She took off her hat and shook out her damp hair. And she smiled.

The Egyptians were all around an exhausted mare who had just given birth. The foal was staggering about on shaking legs. They had been at it all night. She had stroked the mare's forehead, soothing it with soft words. The beast had been worked near death and now the owner nagged them asking over and over when she would be ready to work again. 'If she don't work, I starve. My family starve.' The Egyptian vet, ably assisted by a slim Pakistani man on leave from his own country, interested in setting up a similar operation there, said in Arabic, 'Look, we will give you a small subsistence allowance. Some dinari.' The man's face lit up and he grabbed the vet's hand and kissed it. 'Thank you. Thank you,' he cried.

'But you must do as we tell you,' the vet insisted, 'otherwise no dinari.'

'Oh yes. Oh yes.'

'She must rest in the shade.' He indicated the mare and the man looked blank, bewildered. If he did not take a rest why should the horse? What nonsense was this? 'We insist. Otherwise no dinari.'

The man sighed, looked wildly about as if for help, then giving up to these crazy people he

181

nodded. 'Right. Right.'

'Do you not see?' the Egyptian vet called Suliman asked. 'She will be more use to you, be able to do more work, give you more foals if she is well and strong? Do you not see?' The man nodded but did not look at all sure.

They were packing up to go, cleaning up, putting equipment into the mobile van.

'Did you understand?' the vet asked Perdita and the Pakistani. They nodded. Both had picked up a smattering of the language. 'I never know whether they intend to do as I ask or not,' the Egyptian told Perdita, shaking his head. 'Sometimes they put the unfortunate animal to work directly our back is turned. Sometimes they obey us simply for the money. Then sometimes, Allah be praised, they get the message. They actually see the sense in what I am telling them.'

The foal was greedily sucking from a plastic bottle with a teat the Pakistani was holding out.

'The mother has hardly any milk,' the Egyptian said. 'You'll have to give the foal this.' He gave a box of supplies to the owner.

'Is more than I have for me,' the man said.

'The foal will not live otherwise,' the Egyptian warned the smiling man. 'And it's got stuff in it not right for humans to have,' he added. The man went on smiling. 'He's happy,' the Egyptian remarked laconically to Perdita. 'He thinks he has had great good fortune. It's quite possible he'll use the food for the animals

182

for himself and his family. The money will go, and then . . .' he shrugged, 'who knows?'

'Can't we come back? Monitor him?' Perdita asked.

'We will when we can afford to. That we will leave to you. You have to arrange the money for us to buy the vans and the equipment,' he smiled at her and threw his bag into the back of the van. 'Raising funds so that we can do the job properly.' He too wiped his forehead with his arm, 'Come on. Let's pack it up here. We've done all we can.'

She would delegate. In the summer, in the hot season she would nag the rich, get princes and princesses interested, do the social thing. She would use her father mercilessly. She would get tennis stars, hot from Wimbledon, to open fêtes, opera stars from Glyndebourne and Covent Garden to sing their hearts out at soirées in the gardens of aristocratic houses, and pop singers to rock and roll in the grounds of stately homes. She would get fashion designers to contribute to charity shows on catwalks in grand hotels and top models to give their time free. After all, as her father had said, show them a picture of a wounded animal and they'll give you the moon.

Then in the autumn she would return here, to Egypt and help out, work hard. Winter and spring she would spend here, where her heart was.

Perhaps that was the purpose of Larry

Burton in her life. The reason she had met him. To bring her here, to show her a way of life that she responded to, that she loved. Give her a purpose. If so it had been worth it, all the pain, all the hurt, all the agony.

The others were in the truck. The horse owner was nodding and still smiling at them. She jumped in after them. 'All aboard,' she cried banging the side of the vehicle with her fist. 'C'mon. Let's go, go, go!'

CHAPTER TWENTY-ONE

She got back just in time, two days before the wedding in fact. She suffered through the ceremony, decked out in pink frills. She felt acutely uncomfortable.

She saw it done. Pledges were made and all she could hope to do was get over it and get on with her life.

The final irony that day was when Posy threw her bouquet and Perdita was the one who caught it. It was reflex action, her catching it, she didn't mean to, but there it was in her hands and she could only stand looking silly in the unsuitable fluffy dress.

And David was not there. Nor Fern. She had supper with Leonard that evening, after the feast where she didn't eat anything at all and got tipsy. Leonard said some solid food in her stomach would fix her, so after the speeches, after the toasts, after the bride had thrown the bouquet over her shoulder and the happy couple had departed on their honeymoon, Leonard took her to supper.

'Where are they going, Leonard?' she asked. She held her breath. She could not have borne it if he said Egypt.

'Paris, I think,' he replied. He had brought her to a big noisy restaurant, the latest craze, designed like the Pompidou centre, all steel girders and funnels, scaffolding and tables. Waiters rushed about, good-looking young men, most of them drama students waiting for their big chance, a spot on *The Bill* or a bit in *London Bridge*. They ordered bruschetta and a green salad. Perdita said she could not manage more but Leonard urged her to eat.

'It will soak up the booze,' he said.

'I'm not drunk!' she protested. 'Well, only a bit sloshed.'

She was absent-minded, chewing on the ciabatta bread.

'You still love him, don't you?' Leonard asked, glancing at her quizzically.

'You asked me that before,' she told him. 'Yes I do! I can't help it.'

'I guess love cannot be turned on and off like a tap,' he remarked, then, without a pause, 'Do you think you could get your dad to use a video I made in Slovenia?' he asked slyly.

She sighed. She thought, *here we go again.*

'Oh, Leonard I can try. I need him now, though, for the Cooke Hospital project. But I tell you what, why don't you come to Aswan, or Karnak with me next trip and make a video there? Father will definitely use that, then you can ask him about the other.'

Leonard nodded eagerly. 'Great idea. When do you go?'

'I've got to see Father first. As soon as possible, Leonard. Can you leave at the drop of a hat?'

'I'm ready when you are. I've had my shots so I'm okay there. I'm trying to break into film reporting. My photography has gone as far as it will go.'

'You've got a show coming up,' she said.

'No, Perdita. You missed it. It was on when you were away.'

'Oops! Sorry!'

'It's okay. So I'm ready when you are.'

'All I need is to see Father and get him to remain involved.'

CHAPTER TWENTY-TWO

Perdita found it was quite easy to draw her father into her schemes. She was not stupid enough to imagine that he did it for her sake, or out of compassion for the animals. He did it because after the transmissions about the workings of the hospitals his ratings had soared.

She had made a video of her own emphasising the English origins of the hospital and how it was the British love of animals that saved the situation. Lucas said it was a good psychological move.

'Inspired, my dear. Let the British public feel they are superior to others and they'll shell out quick enough. Forget the hunt meets, the dog fights, the fact that grown men go out in their health and strength and shoot pretty little birds. Forget the fact that the RSPCA is overworked and understaffed and working all the hours God sends. Oh yes!'

'Oh, Father! Don't be such a cynic,' she admonished.

They were lunching in the Groucho. Lucas was attracting a lot of attention. A few brave people came to his table and he introduced her, quite proudly she thought, as his daughter. The one who was raising the profile of the Cooke Hospitals for Animals.

To her surprise he had phoned her and asked her to lunch soon after her return, a few days after the wedding. She had been going to phone him but his call came first. 'Didn't have time to talk to you at Posy's bash,' he said on the phone. She was about to say, no you were too busy! She wondered whether he had screwed Vicky that day or if all those bimbos were red herrings to distract from Fern and his liaison with her. 'I got your letters and your video,' he said, not waiting for her comment, 'but I need a better quality of film. Your video is all very well but it reeks amateur. There are some questions I need to ask you for follow-up, so will you have lunch with me?'

She readily agreed. He was waiting at the table. He rose when she entered and stared at her as if seeing her for the first time. She thought he was going to whistle, his admiration was that obvious.

'God, you look great.' She nodded coolly and sat down, unfazed. She was delighted by his reaction but was not about to let him see that she was.

'The tan suits you,' he said, 'but not when you are decked out in pink frills.'

'The climate played havoc with my skin,' she said. But she knew she looked great. She still wore the same uniform: designer jeans, a sea-island Ralph Lauren cotton shirt the collar turned up near her tanned face and a Hermes scarf knotted at her throat. The sun had bleached her hair platinum and she had a navy cashmere cardigan, its arms tied over her shoulders.

'I want you on the show with me,' he stated baldly, forking green salad into his mouth. She giggled. 'What's so funny?' he asked her suspiciously.

'You look like the cows on the hills,' she laughed, conscious she was annoying him, 'your mouth full of green, chewing!'

He licked it all in glaring at her, but he said nothing.

'Why do you want me on the programme with you?' she asked. 'Aren't you afraid I'll steal the limelight?'

He laughed, genuinely amused. The idea was absurd. No one could steal Lucas Hastings's limelight. 'Because it would be great. Don't you see? Lucas Hastings's daughter following in the footsteps of her old man, up to her ears in social causes, just like him. Noble family, intent on doing good.'

'*A* cause, Father. One!'

'Sure. Animal rights. Flavour of the month. Women's Rights, Ethnic Minorities and Animal Rights. They are the buzz topics of the moment.'

'So you'll use me as a career asset?' she queried.

He nodded. 'Sure,' he replied, unconcerned, 'suits both of us.'

She had to agree.

They talked about a format, surprised that they seemed so much in agreement. When they had finished their rack of lamb, new potatoes and peas, Lucas, not bothering to ask her if she'd like pudding, ordered coffee, sat back and said suddenly, his face serious, not meeting her eyes, 'I think you ought to go and see your mother.'

Surprised, she asked, 'Why?'

'David's been busy while you've been away,' he replied dryly, 'that's why.'

'Da-vid?' she stammered.

'Yes, David! You know. The chap you told I was his father.' He glared at her now, mood quite different, brows drawn together fiercely. 'Chatty, aren't you? Couldn't keep your trap shut. That's why he wasn't at the wedding. He knew I'd be there.'

'I'm sorry, Father. I didn't mean to tell him, truly I didn't. But he was making a move on me. I *had* to.' She kept her voice calm and reasonable.

His eyes widened. 'Oh! Jesus!' Obviously the thought had not struck him before, that such an eventuality was possible. Lucas Hastings was fazed. 'Oh, Christ!'

'Yes, Father. Oh Christ! What was I to do?'

'Lie,' he said briskly.

'Lies don't come so easily to me,' she retorted. He made a face.

'Miss Goodie-two-shoes.'

'No, I'm not. Liars, in my experience reap what they sow and the truth almost always comes out in the end.'

'How true,' he replied sarcastically. 'I suppose you are thinking of me and Fern.'

'Among others!'

'Ah, yes. Posy and Larry. What a to-do, eh?'

'Is David very upset?' she asked, not wanting to talk about Larry.

'David?' he cried as if David's feelings were

190

of little importance in the scheme of things. 'The thing is, yes, David *is* upset. But more important he's rampaging all over town mouthing off, telling all who'll listen about me and Fern Morrison.'

'Can you blame him?'

'Well, yes I can. More diplomacy is needed. After all it is his mother we're talking about here. She's taking it quite well. You see, Paul is dying. He's out of it. Doesn't know day from night and that was her main concern, not to hurt him.'

'Really? Then she should have stopped screwing you all those years.'

'Don't be coarse, Perdita. Much you know of love!'

'Oh but I do, Father, I do.'

He looked at her keenly narrowing his eyes. Then he continued. 'When Paul . . . goes . . .' he hesitated.

'*Dies*, Father. When he dies. Why can't you say it? *When he dies*.'

'I'll move in with her. David shot his bolt, coming the high and mighty, blabbing judgementally all over the place. He's given us the courage to go ahead. It's not what he intended at all but there's nothing to lose now.' He stared at her, then continued. 'I'm not apologising to you or anyone, Perdita.' He paused, stirring his coffee. 'The thing is, with David spewing forth the gutter press are bound to get wind of it and start digging, so I decided to go to them before they "did" me.' He took a deep breath. 'I gave the *Echo* the full exclusive. Shock-horror details. You're not going to like it Perdita but it can't be helped. I slanted it obviously in my favour and I'm afraid your mother and grandfather don't come out of it too well. After all, I've loved Fern for a very long time. I wanted to tell you before they publish.'

'Well, how thoughtful of you!'

'I didn't want you to read it. Not that you'd read that rag, but, well someone would have been sure to show it to you.'

'Why do you suddenly want me to see Mother?' she asked, suddenly realising where this was all leading.

'Ah, yes! Well, Perdita, your mother is very upset. As I said she doesn't come out of it too well,' he looked shifty.

'You mean you told them she got pregnant with me and you *had* to marry her. Oh, Father!' Her voice dripped contempt.

'So she's very upset,' he pressed on, 'very, very upset. I hoped you could talk to her. Console her. I've never hated Melinda, I just don't love her.'

'You could have fooled me! And my mother, in case you hadn't noticed, Father, doesn't *like* me so I can't think she'd be glad to see me. But I'll give it a go.' She stared at him a moment. 'I suppose this is why you want me on the programme? Because the story is about to

192

break. You want me to appear as the loving daughter. Win support. Make you look good.'

He had the grace to look embarrassed, squirming a little. She smiled.

'Don't worry, Father. I'll do it. But not to save your hide. Not for your further glory but because it suits me. I need your help for this thing, otherwise you could go whistle.'

'I said you were a chip.' He grinned at her appreciatively, but she contradicted him.

'No, Father, I'm not. This is not self-interest. This is a cause I'm deeply committed to.'

'Don't kid yourself, honey. I started that way too. And I'm interested in every issue I take up. I could not, *would* not come across believably if I was not. The camera *knows*. But I'm not hypocritical enough to lie and say I don't enjoy what I do, or pretend I'm so lacking in selfishness that I care only about the subject matter. I'll do everything and anything to further my career.'

'How's Miranda taking it?' Perdita asked.

'Surprisingly enough she's fine. She's absorbed in her art. She wants to be a painter. She's good too. I think she guessed about me and her mother a long time ago. Girls are much more practical about things like this.'

'Really?'

'It doesn't seem that important to her, but you never can tell. She's in France at the moment on an art course in Provence. We'll know more when she comes back.'

'Okay, Father, when do you want to do this?'

'Next week. On the programme. We'll use bits of the video you brought back. But you know, Perdita, at some point I'd like a professional film of it all out there . . .'

It gave her great pleasure to announce, 'I have that lined up already.'

'Have you now? Who have you lined up pray?' He looked surprised.

'Leonard Dalton. The photographer.'

'I know who he is. Well done, Perdita. He's a talented chap. That sounds very interesting. Very.' He looked at her. 'You know Perdita, sometimes you amaze me.'

'I know.'

'I've been a lousy father, haven't I?' he asked ruefully.

'Yes,' she said.

'Mmm. Not in my nature. I haven't been any better to David and Miranda.' He made a face. 'I don't like kids,' he said, 'I'm awkward with them.' Then he smiled deprecatingly at her. 'Sorry.'

'It's all right, Father.'

'I must have done something right. You've turned out okay!'

She rose. 'Well, Father, thanks for lunch. I'll be in touch.' She turned to go but he called her and looking back at him over her shoulder she caught his appreciative, buccaneer smile. 'And Perdita, you've turned into a stunner. I thought you ought to know.'

194

She grinned back at him. 'I do know,' she said. 'It's a little late though, Father. You should have told me that years ago, no matter whether it was true or not. But you never really saw me, did you?'

'No, and I was a fool,' he said and watched her as she walked away head held high.

Perdita went to see her mother. Melinda was not at the Design Factory. They said there that she was 'at home' and Perdita took that to mean the apartment in Kensington. However, her mother was not there either, so Perdita drove to Oak Wood Court.

She felt curiously calm and cheerful as she sped along the motorway. Autumn was in full and gloriously strident colour, the red and gold, burnt umber and copper of the leaves glowing warmly in the burnished sunlight. She thought of the many journeys she had made down this road in fear and apprehension, nervous and unsure. Well, not any more. Her parents no longer had the power to hurt her. She had advanced out of their reach.

Oak Wood Court was ablaze with amber glory and she could see the gardener and the handyman busy collecting the fallen leaves. Everything must be tidy for Melinda, Perdita thought. If it was me I'd like to leave them scattered over the earth for a while. She said so to her mother. 'It would be like an exotic carpet.'

Her mother was sipping a hot chocolate on

the terrace. She looked pale but immaculate as usual. She was wrapped in a cashmere housecoat, blue as her eyes.

'Well, when all this is yours you can do what you like, Perdita,' she told her daughter tartly, 'but until then neatness and order is the name of the game, I'm afraid. Your grandfather dinned it into me. Neatness and order.' Then she examined her daughter. 'You look different,' she remarked.

'Father said I looked stunning,' Perdita said.

'Did he now! Oh well, I don't think for a moment he realises what you have done to your skin. You'll look a hundred soon, I wouldn't wonder. Like a crocodile.'

'Thank you, Mother.'

Melinda drummed her fingers, long nails perfectly manicured. 'I suppose you know he's broken my heart,' she stated dramatically. Perdita burst out laughing.

'Oh, Mother!' she cried, 'you're not serious!'

'Don't you *dare* laugh at me,' Melinda said glaring at her angrily. 'He has publicly humiliated and made a complete fool of me before the whole world.' She stared out over the lawn, pulling the robe closer around her. She tapped a newspaper that lay on the table in disarray. The *Echo*.

'Have you seen this?' she asked.

'Yes,' Perdita said, 'I have seen that. But Mother, humiliation and being made a fool of are not the same things as having your heart

196

broken.' I should know, she thought.

Her mother held up the silver pot. 'Some chocolate?' she asked and Perdita nodded. 'Sit down, Perdita. Don't *hover*. It makes me nervous.'

She poured the drink for her daughter and offered Perdita an almond tuille. 'I have lived with your father all these years pretending I didn't know about *her*. It's been a terrible strain.'

Perdita gasped and put her cup down abruptly. Her mother glanced at her.

'You thought I didn't know? You thought I was that stupid? Well, I did know about Fern Morrison.' She spat out the name. 'She's haunted me all my married life. Oh God, Perdita, you have no idea what it is like, three in a marriage. Your lover loving someone else.'

Oh yes I do. Dear God, I do. Perdita sipped her drink. It warmed her. She felt very cold inside.

'Why did you trap him into marriage, Mother? You should have known it wouldn't work.'

'I thought it *would*. I was very young. My father brought me up to believe he could get me anything, make anything I wanted happen. And he could, everything except your father. Oh he got him for me all right. *Purchased* him for me. But he left out the fact that you cannot manipulate human emotions. You can *get* someone but you cannot make them love you. I thought your father would forget Fern and begin to love me. After all I was bringing him so much. This place. A guaranteed career. Young people always believe the impossible. It is hope. I was so crazy about him, you see. I waited and waited and it never happened. I waited until this,' she tapped the paper, 'hoping, endlessly hoping.' There were tears in her eyes. 'I was so much in love. I would have done anything, gone anywhere, followed him to the ends of the earth for one kindness, one endearment.'

I know, oh I know, Mother, Perdita thought, but remained silent.

'But all I brought him made him resent me. The very gifts I brought him poisoned him against me.'

'I think you have to face the fact, Mother, that no matter what you did he wouldn't have been in love with you. You cannot force a man to love you.' As I know. As I know so well.

Melinda sighed, looking out at the massed red-gold trees and a tear fell on her cheek and ran down leaving a little pathway in her make-up. Perdita stared at it. She had never before seen her mother's make-up flawed.

'Oh, but he did love me,' she whispered. 'I had one night of passion with him. One night when he loved me, was all mine. And you were conceived, and so he had to marry me. Father said. He'd have blacklisted him else. He had that power.'

Perdita shook her head. 'I think you are mixing sex up with love, Mother.' Then thought, I don't think she knows the difference. 'But Mother, to trap him like that . . . it wasn't fair.'

'I didn't *care*,' Melinda cried. 'And that one night that he loved me was worth it all, everything I suffered.' I know, Perdita thought, I feel the same about Larry. Oh God, it was worth it.

Melinda turned back to Perdita, 'This will all be yours when I die. I don't want Lucas involved.'

It had never before occurred to Perdita that eventually she would be mistress of Oak Wood Court and she was not at all sure she wanted to be. It had never felt like home to her. It was not a place she felt comfortable in.

'Don't, Mother. For Goodness' sake, that shouldn't be an issue for a long long time.'

'Oh yes it is. I've got cancer Perdita. I've a year at most.'

Perdita's eyes widened. Her mother had never been close to her but *death*! Unable to absorb the implications of this information she listened in silence as her mother continued, 'I filed for divorce while you were away. I'll get it very soon. It will come through any day now. And I've made a will. It's airtight, says *everything* of mine, this house, this land, my money, is all yours and Lucas can't touch a penny. My lawyers assure me he has no claim.

199

Not since he went into print about his unfaithfulness.'

'Mother, I don't *want* it. Don't you see?' Perdita looked earnestly at her mother. 'It would be a repetition of your mistake.'

'What?' Melinda looked puzzled.

'Don't you understand, Mother? You've led a life of bitterness and frustration. For years and years now, decades you have destroyed yourself, been eaten up, doing what? Waiting. Waiting for something to change. My father married you only because of me and because of all this,' she swept her arm around indicating the land, the mansion behind them. 'And you and he both suffered because your priorities were all wrong. Suffered endlessly. Because of this place. Without all this you would both have broken away. Father would have gone to Fern, lived with her and his family there. He'll be so happy, doing that.'

'Well, I don't want him to be happy.'

'Then you don't love him, Mother. It's what made him so bitter and hateful, all those years loving someone else. Not being able to love her publicly, not being able to acknowledge the kids. And you, Mother, who knows? You might have found another love. Another life.'

Melinda stubbornly shook her head. 'No. I've always been mad about Lucas. There would never have been another man for me.'

'That's being close-minded. You don't *know*. People change. In any event you could have

200

had a happier life. Even alone. Free to do as you wished, Mother, not mentally tied to a man who did not love you.' She thought, I could be talking about myself. This could be me if I hadn't got the project. Am I so like her then? We are both one-man women. 'And I don't want that legacy, Mother. I don't want all these accoutrements. Not knowing if the one I loved loved me for myself or all this *stuff*! Look at Posy Gore. It took me so long to realise all she fell for was what we had.' Perdita shook her head, narrowing her eyes against the glare of the autumn sun, sipping her chocolate. 'I was never popular in school, Mother. And it was because of this. I wish, I just wish I had been ordinary. Not hampered by too many possessions and parents so much in the spotlight. You have to be very strong to survive that. And you flaunted the possessions. So did Gramps.' She looked at Melinda, shrinking deeper into her housecoat. Her mother looked suddenly frail. 'There was a poem we did at school Mother. William Henry Davies. End of term concert. You and Father were supposed to be there when I recited it all by myself up on the stage. But you never came.' She closed her eyes, remembering that small figure, red knees, scanning the audience, hoping, praying, then realising no one of hers was there. Other girls waved surreptitiously to loved and familiar faces, but there was no one there for her to wave to. Vicky Mendel whispering, 'Your dad

201

so high and mighty he thinks school concerts beneath him?'

Had Miss Davenport deliberately chosen that particular poem for her to recite? Or had it been the luck of the draw, a haphazard choice? She recited it again now, not caring any more whether her mother listened or not.

"When I had money, money, O!
I knew no joy till I was poor;
For many a false man as a friend
Came knocking all day at my door."

'Posy,' her mother interjected, 'I never liked that girl.'

"Much have I thought of life, and seen
How poor men's hearts are ever light,
And how their wives do hum like bees
About their work from morn till night."

'Well, I don't know about *that* Perdita!'
'It was the time Mother, the period. I *know* what it means. Listen,

"So, when I hear these poor ones laugh,
And see the rich ones coldly frown—
Poor men, think I, need not go up
So much as rich men should come down.

When I had money, money, O!
My many friends proved all untrue;
202

But now I have no money, O!
My friends are real, though very few."

'That's what I feel, Mother. So let Lucas have it. Heaven knows he's paid for it. Over and over again. He deserves it, and quite frankly Father doesn't really care if his friends are true or not.'

'That's a terrible thing to say, Perdita!'

'Well, Mother, I'm afraid it's true.'

Nothing Melinda could say would change her daughter's mind. When Melinda told her she would leave the will as it was and Perdita would, willy-nilly, inherit, Perdita said, 'If you do that Mother, I'll sell up, everything and give it to the hospital. Cooke's needs the money more than I do. We could build a whole new hospital in Nepal for what this place would fetch.'

'Oh my God, Perdita, no! That would be terrible.'

'Well, it's your choice, Mother.'

'At the wedding, I was so . . . Oh Perdita, I'm so unhappy. My life's been such a mess.'

For the life of her Perdita could muster no sympathy. Her heart felt dry and cold. She was sorry for her mother, but it was like reading a book. She was not touched.

'Yes, Mother. It has and I don't intend to follow in your footsteps. At least Father grabbed a little joy on the side. Let him have the damned place.'

Perdita stayed with her mother, talking to her, being supportive, but more like a nurse than a daughter. She did not, could not pretend a love she did not feel.

Although Melinda clung to her and obviously needed her now it was too late for Perdita. And it was too late for Melinda to change. She remained self-absorbed, never thinking to ask Perdita about her work, the Cooke Hospital, her daughter's interests.

During the last year of her mother's life Perdita was mainly in Egypt. When she came home she spent as much time as she could with Melinda. She was dutiful, sometimes flying from Egypt to spend a long weekend with her mother. But she did not pretend a grief she did not feel and when Melinda died the following autumn at Oak Wood Court her daughter was at her side. But she did not cry at the funeral.

By then Perdita's life had changed completely and as she gazed at her mother's coffin being lowered into the earth she was engulfed by a great sadness at the waste of a life, a life that repelled love, rejected affection and died waiting for something that could not, never would happen.

CHAPTER TWENTY-THREE

Leonard went with her to Karnak. She had done the show with her father and the studio had been inundated with phone calls and overwhelmed with letters, faxes, e-mail and cheques. It was a huge success.

Perdita advertised for a secretary and gave the job to a young man called Malcolm Radcliffe. He had been accountant for the NSPCA, was passionate about animals and was very rich. A minor member of the aristocracy, he was inhibited, had a stammer and was painfully shy. Perdita warmed to him instantly. He was very like what she had been.

The Cooke Hospital project was perfect for him as it had been for her and, unlike her, Malcolm had spent his whole life with animals.

'I like them better than humans,' he told her, 'they're reliable. They don't desert you, don't make fun of you, and they never let you down. No, they're much better people than people.'

Perdita laughed. 'I do know what you mean, Malcolm, but I only ever had a dog and a cat. You've farmed.'

'My father farmed,' he told her, 'and the farm went to my big brother. I spent all my life fighting fox-hunting. All the excuses are a total lie. It is cruel beyond belief. As Oscar Wilde said, "The unspeakable in pursuit of the uneatable".'

Perdita left all the book-keeping to him, 'It's not glamorous, your side of the business, doing the accounts,' she said.

'I don't mind. Anything that helps. Only too glad.'

'You can come out and see our operations

205

for yourself when you've finished that lot.' She pointed to the racks of mail to be answered, the faxes, the cheques to be acknowledged and receipted, the thank-yous to everybody.

'Oh gosh! Golly! Good. I'd love that.'

'We are a small, dedicated team,' she told him, not informing him that the small dedicated team had two members not on speaking terms, who communicated by fax and who spent a great deal of energy avoiding each other.

'That suits me fine,' he said and gave his neighing laugh and Perdita thought, not for the first time that he was exactly like a horse.

Leonard said, 'I think his Mater had an affair with a stallion and Malcolm is the result,' and Perdita told him to try to be sensitive to the newcomer.

'He's been scarred,' she told him. 'Takes one to know one.'

'Yeah! I know the sort. His Mater threw him into boarding school when he was six and . . .'

'Yes, Leonard. So watch what you say. No taking the mickey, okay.'

'Okay. You're the boss!'

'I like him,' she added, watching Malcolm sorting the mail with precise efficiency.

'Yeah, so do I. But he's just like a horse. Equine. Tosses his head. Laughs like a nag and moves like a colt. He's probably gay.'

Perdita did not care whether he was or not. He did a superb job and was a thoughtful employee, always available, always enthusiastic.

In Egypt she laboured. She worked until she dropped. Yasser was a constant support and help and together they not only made the units in Karnak, Edfu and Luxor solvent, but where there had been only one hospital on the outskirts of Cairo, there was now the beginnings of what would be, as the funds came in, another quite large one in the centre of the city.

She kept out of Larry's way. Yasser told her he was in Luxor three weeks after his wedding day.

'Is he alone?' she asked.

He nodded. 'Yes. His wife is not with him.'

'What does he propose to do?'

'He wants to go to Jordan. He asked me if you were going there. He said if you were he would come here to Cairo instead. I told him I would ask you.' Yasser looked at her, his large brown eyes reproachful. 'I told him I did not like being used like this. As a go-between,' he spread his hands. 'It's not dignified.'

'I'm sorry, Yasser, and you are quite right. We cannot avoid each other forever.'

Yasser paused, then glanced at her under his bushy brows. 'He asked, like you did, if you were alone.'

'What did you say?'

He smiled wickedly. 'I said you had Leonard with you.'

She giggled. 'Oh, Yasser, you are naughty!' But she worried about meeting him.

Sometimes it was too hot to sleep and she lay awake all night listening to the night noises, the constant hum of activity on the banks of the Nile, the sound of the overhead fan in her room purring softly, until eventually the high, harsh call to prayer from the mezzuin came from the minarets announcing that it was dawn. It was a record now, not a person any more and she thought sadly that progress left many casualties.

She thought about Larry all the time. It was as if he'd left her for a while and would be back any minute to take her in his arms and kiss her and make love to her and she thought, I'm exactly like Mother. If I'm not careful I'll waste my life marking time. Dreaming instead of living.

*   *   *

Leonard made a magnificent documentary about the animal hospitals in Egypt. Full of poignant images and wonderful enthusiasm he had brought all his skill as a photographer to bear and the result was stunning. He used both herself and Larry, but separately and although they never met, on tape it appeared they did.

Lucas was delighted with Leonard's work and predicted it would be nominated for awards.

Paul Morrison mercifully died and, after the funeral, Lucas moved into the house with Fern. Miranda seemed unconcerned, accepting her mother's behaviour with absent-minded indulgence. Utterly absorbed in her own life, she behaved as if Lucas was simply another lodger in place of Paul. She seemed to care little who was *in situ*.

'The young are so preoccupied with themselves, their own lives, their own affairs,' Lucas told Perdita, 'it amazes me.'

'Does it, Father? I think your statement applies to the older generation as well.' Her tone was caustic.

'Oh, Perdita, you enchant me! You are developing a witty style all your own.'

He was proud of her, she realised and in her long and affectionless life it was better than nothing. A distinct change for the better.

She pondered the fact that when she ceased to need their love, both parents had developed an affection for her.

David had not taken the situation as calmly as his sister. He was angry and hurt and Perdita hoped that Larry was helping him.

He had moved into Larry's rooms over the surgery and although Perdita tried to talk to him on the phone he brushed her off briskly and made it obvious he did not want to have any more to do with her than he had to.

In the spring before her mother died Perdita, flying home from Egypt for the weekend to see her, found Posy Burton at Oak Wood Court. Perdita was tired, dusty and hungry, not at all pleased when on running up the steps to the terrace where she could see her mother swathed in her cashmere shawls, sipping tea, she realised Melinda was not alone. There was someone else sitting in the pristine-white high-backed wicker chair in the shadows. As she kissed her mother the shadow rose and Perdita, turning, saw it was Posy.

'Hello Perdy.'

Perdita was silent a moment, collecting herself. She had not seen Posy since her wedding day.

Posy looked slim and svelte. She had an elegance about her, a well-groomed, pampered patina that made the viewer look twice. She had stopped bleaching and flattening her hair to look like Perdita and it was her natural soft brown colour springing out in a cloud about her face, making her features look small and dainty. She looked very pretty and all Perdita could feel was a terrible resentment.

She must be happy with Larry, she thought angrily. Then, sadly, he must love her. She has the look of a woman in love. That look had not been there on her wedding day. Strange.

Perdita nodded to her friend. 'Hi Posy!' she said a trifle sullenly. 'Mother, how are you? You mustn't tire yourself.'

'I won't tire her Perdy,' Posy said.

'I'm *not* tired,' her mother protested

210

peevishly, 'I'm full of drugs and I'm feeling no pain. For the moment.'

Melinda's face was egg-shell pale, her cheeks sunken, her eyes panda-circled. She wore a turban to hide her hair, thinning now from the chemotherapy.

'Mother, I . . .'

'No go! Go walk with Posy. She wants to talk to you.' Melinda lay back on the reclining canvas chair they had got for her.

'Oh, does she? About what may I ask?' Perdita knew she sounded childishly sarcastic but she could not help herself.

'About Larry,' Posy said tranquilly.

'Well, I've nothing to say to you on that score, Posy, so you can save your breath.'

'I think you might have,' Melinda waved a hand aimlessly in the air. 'Go on. Go to the cherry orchard. See the trees in bloom. They are a wonderful sight.'

Reluctantly, Perdita went. Posy walked beside her but did not take her arm as she used to in the old days. The trees were shedding clouds of moon-silver petals and the glittering shower like snow peppered the girls' hair. The pale spring sun glimmered through the trees.

'When all the world was young, Perdy, we used to walk like this. Under these trees.'

Perdita closed her eyes, then said, 'I was a fool ever to trust you Posy. You sucked me dry.'

To her surprise, Posy nodded. 'I know,' she said, 'and I'm sorry.'

211

'Bit late for that. Everyone is sorry all of a sudden. Father, Mother. Now you. And it's too late, Posy. It's too late.'

Posy shook her head. 'It's never too late, Perdy.' She stopped and turned, looking around. 'There used to be a bench here somewhere.' Spotting it, she said, 'Ah, here it is. Let's sit.'

She sat down, seemingly not worried about the seat of her beige suit. Perdita stood over her. 'Look here, Posy, I'm tired and travel-stained. I need a shower and something to eat. This is not a good time to exchange reminiscences. If you think I'm going to park myself here and natter to you about the past and your marriage you are very much mistaken.' I sound exactly like Father, she thought.

'Oh, sit down, Perdy and shut up and listen,' Posy commanded irritably. 'God, you can be very uppity. Arrogant. You always were. Making it impossible for people to get near you.'

She was probably right, Perdita decided ruefully and sat. Her jeans had protected her from much worse than the lichen-encrusted bench.

'I'm in love, Perdy. For the first time in my life. Truly in love.'

Oh God! Oh God! Perdita's heart sank and she felt suddenly sick and faint. 'I don't want to hear this, Posy,' she almost begged.

212

'Oh yes you do!'

'Why are you being so cruel?' she whispered helplessly.

'Ah! So you do still love him?'

Perdita did not reply, she did not have to. Posy smiled at her. 'This is the first decent thing I've ever done for you, isn't it?'

'I don't understand.'

'Larry is yours, Perdita. He always was, always will be.'

'But you love him.'

'No. Not Larry. Listen, Perdy, I confess. I've always been envious of you, of what you had. All this.' She looked at the blossom-laden branches of the cherry trees laced overhead, the outline of Oak Wood Court in the shimmering distance. 'A distinguished and famous father. A fun mother . . .'

'Fun!' Perdita echoed in disbelief, but her mind was trying to get around those sentences Posy had just uttered: *Larry is yours.* How could he be? He was married to Posy. She had been at the ceremony, a witness.

'And you were beautiful,' Posy was saying, 'the other girls were so jealous. So was I.'

'This is all in the past, Posy. Over and forgotten.'

'No, it's not. I wanted to be like you Perdy, *be* you, so I changed my hair colour and copied your clothes. I wormed my way into your mother's affections and then into a job with her company. It was so easy.'

213

'I never could. Worm my way into her affections, I mean.'

'No. You couldn't, could you?'

'Where's all this leading, Posy? You're not telling me anything I don't already know.'

'It's leading me to telling you that I stole Larry too. I lied to him. Said I was pregnant when I wasn't. I seduced him, Perdy, told him I was going to have his baby.'

'And he fell for it?' Perdita's voice was bitter.

'You know Larry, Perdita. An honourable man. There are not many of his kind left. He would never leave a child of his without a proper and legitimate father, and of course he believed me. He *would*. I was very persuasive. And Larry is not the sort of chap to go about suspicious of people. Like you, he *trusts*. Stupid, if you ask me.'

Perdita stared at her. 'He realised his mistake almost at once.' Posy bit her lip. 'I was so disgusted with myself. Copying your clothes, your hair was one thing. Stealing from you was another.' Perdita looked at her in surprise. 'Oh yes, I took things from you too,' she said, 'I took lots of things without telling you. Cardigans. Perfume. Soap. Scarves.'

'I thought I was careless, always losing things.'

'I let you think that. And coaxing your mother, well, it was childish at best. But Larry was another matter altogether and I regretted it almost at once.'

214

'You seemed to enjoy your wedding,' Perdita could not keep the bitterness out of her voice.

'Yes I did. I would be lying if I said I didn't. It was great, sitting there on the top table, all in white, the cynosure of all eyes. I had achieved what I had set out to do. I had *won*.' She laughed. 'You looked so silly in that pink and suddenly for the first time in my life I felt equal. I had a man *you* wanted. I was the star attraction. I looked as good as you.'

She turned away. 'Then we were alone together and it all collapsed. It was shocking and sordid.'

She paused and Perdita could see her chewing her lip. She used to do that in school when she was upset and Perdita used to tell her to stop but she never did.

'We arrived that night in Paris. Larry had been so silent on the plane. He couldn't make love to me, Perdy. He just couldn't bring himself to. He tried, but it was no use. The same sense of honour that forced him to marry me when he thought I was pregnant, the morality that insisted he give his child a stable home, that very virtue forbade him having sex with someone he did not love. He could not be unfaithful to you.'

She paused then, 'You see when he'd . . . no, he *didn't* make love to me that time, before. When we came back from Oak Wood Court. Remember the night? I insisted on cadging a lift? I made love to *him*, took him by storm. But

215

that was before you two were *really* serious, before you went to Egypt. After he had pledged himself to you it became impossible for him.' She paused again. 'It was a farce. We were strangers. He was fair and said he'd make a stab at some kind of life together. For the child's sake. But I wasn't pregnant. I felt degraded. No triumph now. So I told him the truth.'

Another pause. Then, 'We were sitting at a sidewalk café. You know those Parisian cafés? It was autumn, remember. The trees were glorious and there was a snap in the air, like energy. Exciting. All around us people were talking. You know the way they do in France, gesticulating, waving their arms about, fluttering their hands, chatting nineteen to the dozen, laughing, being affectionate, touching each other. Smooching. Oh, everyone seemed to me to be in love. And Larry and I sat silent as the grave. Nothing to say. Nothing at all. We sat at either side of the table, silently sipping our *café au lait*, staring into space. There was no victory there, just boredom. So I told him the truth. That I'd planned it. The seduction. That I wanted what you had. That I wasn't pregnant.' She glanced at Perdita. 'I'll never forget his face, the way he looked at me. The loathing. The contempt. I was lower than the lowest in his eyes. That honourable man could not comprehend such perfidity, not in a million years. To him I was a malignant and worthless

216

sub-human. He stared at me for a long moment, that look upon his face, then he left. Stood up, put some francs on the table and went. I never saw him again.'

They sat in silence while Perdita tried to sort out her feelings. At first she had briefly decided that if he was weak enough to be seduced by Posy and silly enough to believe she was pregnant, then he did not deserve her love. She was too good for him. But it was typical of Larry that he would feel that if he fathered a child he must marry the mother, and it was his utterly chivalrous and noble character, his very old-fashioned morals that had made her love him so much. She could not blame him then if he acted in character.

Posy was right. He was an honourable man and not many women in these times thought that admirable. But she did. Oh yes, she did.

Posy said, 'When I got back to the hotel his clothes, his suitcases were there. He never retrieved them. Couldn't bear to. He'd paid the hotel by credit card. They said he'd phoned through. He vanished from my life, Perdita. All over.'

'That was . . . when?' Perdita asked.

'Autumn last year. I thought he might come back to me. Get over his disgust. Also I did not want to admit I'd been dumped.' A smile broke, like sun coming out from behind a cloud and her face softened. 'Then last month something happened to me to change

217

everything.'

'You said you were in love. I thought you meant . . .'

'Oh God, no!' Posy laughed, 'no. It's David. David Morrison, Larry's partner. And from what the papers say, your half-brother. He consoled me when I tried to find Larry. He was so good to me.'

'He seems to make a habit of that,' Perdita muttered. She rose and paced about trying to work it out, thinking.

'Well,' Posy asked eventually, 'what do you think, Perdy?'

'It's another part of me, Posy. Just another part of *me*. Don't you see that? You seem unable to go outside my family. It's the same old pattern.'

'But I love him. It is different, Perdy. When I came back from Paris alone I was miserable for a while. I couldn't go to you and I had no one else. Mother and Father are in Columbia. I think Father's been demoted. He's in a terribly nervous state and my mother is off the walls. Well, anyhow I decided to sue for divorce.'

'It was too soon surely?'

Posy shook her head. 'No. On the grounds of non-consummation. He's never made love to me, had sex with me *after* the ceremony. I went to the surgery to try and talk to Larry about it, ask his forgiveness and I met David. Well, we talked. About you. About Larry. We were both angry and we found it a relief to share our

218

resentments. Well, the long and the short of it is, Perdy, we plan to marry as soon as my divorce comes through.'

'So where has David been all this time?' Perdita asked.

'Why, with me!'

Perdita stared at her friend. No matter how hard she tried she could find no affection in her heart for Posy. But she had no hatred either, she simply felt sorry for her. Posy doing the same immature things as she had always done.

'So I'll be Lucas Hastings's daughter-in-law,' she said now, smiling at Perdita.

'Yes, Posy, you will.' She was glowingly happy, that was obvious.

She rose and took Perdita's hand. 'And everything is okay now? I've made amends. And we're truly sisters at last, Perdy. Isn't that grand?'

Perdita didn't reply.

'And I'll help you with the project, Perdy. I've seen it on *Hastings Hour*. I'll get into it with David and we'll be a team.'

Perdita thought for a moment. Her first reaction was dread. Posy interfering again, perhaps making trouble. But on second thoughts she realised such a thing was impossible. Posy had no power over her any longer and she had so alienated Larry as to make herself obnoxious to him. She could imagine his reaction and how he now felt about Posy. Perdita had, by now, authority enough in the organisation to control what Posy did. She would not enjoy the field work in Egypt, that was certain. Posy was not one to tolerate the harsh conditions Perdita accepted as part of the job. No, she would give Posy to Malcolm and, knowing Malcolm, he would put Posy to work slaving over a hot computer, answering letters and phone calls. It was not Posy's style. She was too ambitious for Cooke's Animal Hospital. She'd love to appear on TV but would be in the bar hob-nobbing with the media names, not at all interested in the results of the transmission. That part of the operation would bore her to death. So would the heat, the flies, the medical requirements. No, Perdita reflected, Posy could not, would not disturb her any more. She had no power over her and, Perdita thought, I'm free. At last I'm really free. And she smiled to herself as Posy rambled on.

She rose and, gently removing Posy's hand from her arm, she walked beside her back to the house.

*   *   *

Perdita was lying on her bed in the Old Cataract Hotel, drenched in sweat. The dark wood fan overhead turned swiftly and silently trying to circulate the stagnant air. She stared at it mindlessly.

She was very tired. A lot had happened to occupy her mind. The new hospital in Cairo was well under way but more money was needed. It would probably always be like that.

Leonard was working on another programme to be shown before Christmas. She was in daily communication with Malcolm and Posy who had settled down obediently under David's wing. Lucas said he'd work in the latest video because, he said, in January and February people did not want to spend. 'We'll have to show it before Christmas. People are more disposed then to spend. With Christmas over generosity flies out the window.'

Her father seemed younger, more boyish and certainly more cheerful during the past year. He had stood beside her at Melinda's funeral. 'Poor cow!' he'd whispered. 'Poor sad cow. What a drag she was.'

'Father, don't be unkind. Not now,' she'd whispered back and he'd lapsed into silence.

He was happy with Fern and Perdita had formed a tentative friendship with her father's mistress, soon to be wife. She liked Fern and got on well with her when the emotional baggage was unpacked, discussed and sorted.

She remained close, too, to Anjelica Burton. Larry's mother had called her and invited her to stay at the cottage. Perdita had confided everything to her and she had sighed and quoted, '"Oh what a tangled web we weave when first we practise to deceive"! Oh, my dear, I hope you will not allow my son's old-fashioned morals to keep you two apart. You are so very right for each other.' She leaned over to the girl. 'And you know, Perdita, if you had been in Larry's shoes you'd have done the same. You too are honourable. When you are discrediting your mother and father remember we have the morals we are given and it seems to me that, difficult as it may be to credit it, they did not do so bad a job.' When she saw Perdita's surprise she said, 'Oh yes, my dear, they did. And, if you'd got pregnant by, say Leonard even though you loved Larry, you would have felt honour-bound to marry the photographer, wouldn't you? Peas in a pod, oh yes you are, so like each other.'

David and Posy announced they were engaged. Fern was mildly troubled, but she had Lucas there to support her now and it was Lucas who said, 'Don't worry, I'll keep that young lady in line. I have her working her guts out in the studios. I know what makes her tick. Just throw a big name at her for ten minutes every now and then and she's happy. I'll see David comes to no harm.' And both Perdita and Fern believed him.

In the meantime there was her work. It occupied her thoughts, took all her energy. Gave her all her energy.

And now, in the hotel in Egypt she decided it was useless trying to sleep. She got up, showered and slipping into a loose silk wrap, she opened the French windows, went out on the balcony and looked up at the sky.

She never ceased to marvel at the density of the stars here in the desert. There seemed to be so many more visible here than in England. Clotted together in massy brilliance, they danced in and out in glittering splendour. The sky looked like a dark cloak trailing diamonds.

Everything was quiet now, between the night and the dawning, the world hesitating between night and day.

She stretched her arms wide and drew in a breath of cold morning air. She could smell the desert, that dry hot smell and the fragrance of the fig trees, the olive groves near the banks of the Nile. She sniffed the ancient river itself, sour and salty. She thought of Cleopatra and Nefertiti, Hatshepsut and the fabled beauty of the women of Egypt. They must have stared as she was doing at the slow green waters and the twinkling stars.

'You take my breath away.'

The soft voice came from under the palm tree in the midia n that divided the toing and froing traffic on the street. But she knew that voice. That voice had never been far from her heart.

Her heart leapt within her and she dared not breathe. The figure detached itself. 'Larry,' she cried, leaning down, her face illuminated by the stars and her love. 'Wait,' she called, 'wait there.'

She ran inside, got the hotel key with the room number on it. She leaned over the balcony and threw the key to him. A drowsy driver with his donkey and trap looked at them sleepily, then laughed.

Larry caught the key and disappeared. She went inside and closed the windows.

There would be no recriminations. There would be no hashing and rehashing of the past. Their love was stronger than that, purer and more enduring.

As the door opened she too opened her arms to receive her love, her passion. Larry.